THE CHRISTMAS TREE

By

Breanna Cone

Jann...
Our friendship
doesn't span that
many years but it
is precious to me
love ya
Breanna Cone

This book is a work of fiction. Places, events, and situations in this story are purely fictional. Any resemblance to actual persons, living or dead, is coincidental.

First published by AuthorHouse 04/09/04

ISBN: 1-4140-8605-9 (e-book)
ISBN: 1-4184-2868-X (Paperback)

This book is printed on acid free paper.

PROLOGUE

New York City

The coffee shop across the street from the law offices of Smith and Jones was unusually quiet for the busy holiday season. The tabletop Christmas tree at the end of the counter was gaily decorated with miniature red and gold ornaments. The twinkling lights flashed on and off like a pulse as if they were keeping time with the traffic on the busy street. A tin pail was sitting under the edge of the branches with a sign that asked the patrons to give their tip money to help support a local soup kitchen and food bank.

The small café was a popular haven for the weary 5th Avenue shoppers who needed to rest their feet but today there were only two men sitting in a booth at the back. John Jones and Robert Smith were having their midmorning coffee break but the daily ritual was coming to an end today.

John had started the coffee break tradition more than twenty years ago. He'd wanted to take a break away from the formal atmosphere of the law offices in an effort to make Robert feel more comfortable in his new role as junior partner. The only guidelines were that no current cases or legal business were ever discussed. The time was spent talking about all types of topics ranging from the latest sports fiasco to any personal plans they wanted to share with each other. These few minutes everyday had forged a unique friendship based on respect and loyalty to each other that was rare in their profession.

"Have you made any retirement plans?" Robert asked his old friend. He was going to miss these talks but most of all he would miss this man, who had taught him so much about the practice of law and the meaning of true friendship.

"Mary and I are going to officially open the Good Samaritan Tree Farm. We've been growing fir trees on our property in Connecticut for the past six years. The trees should be ready for the holiday season next year. We're going to donate a dozen trees to local orphanages and nursing homes to be used during the Christmas holidays and the rest will be for sale to the public." John grinned broadly at his table companion's shocked expression. It was rare thing to see him speechless.

"When did you find time and energy for such a major project?" Robert asked in amazement after his brain recovered from the shock of his friend's announcement. If John had said he was going to take ballet lessons or become an astronaut, he couldn't have been more surprised.

"We didn't do the hands on labor ourselves. We consulted a forestry engineer when we first began thinking seriously about a tree farm." John smiled as he related that first meeting with Scott Williams.

The November air was clear and crisp with the smell of wood smoke coming from the fireplace chimney. After the noise of the city, it was a relief to be able to hear birds chirping instead of car horns honking impatiently. John was sitting on the porch, which extended across the front of his country home, drinking a cup of coffee, enjoying the peace and quiet of the country as he waited for the consultant to arrive.

Today, he and Mary were taking the first step toward getting their retirement plans underway. They had researched and made tentative plans for this special project for the past year but they were going to take it from the drawing board into the realm of reality.

A Dodge 4x4 truck slowed then pulled into the drive and parked next to the short walkway leading to the house. A quick glance at his watch confirmed that his guest was on time for his appointment. Punctuality was a good sign because it showed respect for the other person's busy schedule. John watched as a large gentleman got out of the truck and walked up the steps onto the porch. Scott Williams was younger than he had expected but he had come highly recommended as an expert on tree and property development.

"Hello, Mr. Jones. I'm Scott Williams." Scott approached the older man who stood up as he had mounted the steps and shook his hand.

Nice firm handshake. No sweaty palms. That was another good sign. It meant this man had confidence in the knowledge of his chosen field of work and in his ability to convey this to his clients. "Please call me John. Mr. Jones makes me feel like I'm in the courtroom."

John opened the door and motioned him in. The only other occupant of the living room was an attractive lady sitting by the fire quietly observing them.

"Mary, this is Scott Williams. Scott, this is my wife, Mary."

"Good morning, Scott. Welcome to our home." Mary smiled as she stood up to shake the hand he offered. Even though his hand seemed to dwarf hers, his was a gentle touch not the bone-shattering grip she had expected.

Scott looked around in surprise. Instead of the opulence he had expected of a successful corporate attorney's country home, the living room was a cozy area similar to what an average family would own. Two large recliners flanked the fireplace that was ablaze with a welcoming fire. Directly in front of the fireplace was a brown and tan plaid sofa with big, soft cushions that invited you to sit and relax. An entertainment center stood against the wall with a DVD player, a stereo system and a wide screen television for the times when they wanted to connect with the outside world. On a serving cart was a silver coffee service along with a sugar and creamer set.

"Would you like a cup of coffee?" Mary asked this gentle giant of a man.

"Yes. Black, please," Scott replied with quick smile at the graciousness of his hostess.

Scott knew that Mary Williams was probably in her late fifties but her short, brown hair had only a few silver strands. They didn't detract from her looks at all. They complimented a face that was still youthful with just a few laugh lines around her hazel eyes. Those eyes were twinkling merrily as if she had just discovered the answer to a secret riddle.

Mary handed a cup of coffee to Scott and invited him to sit by the fire. She took that opportunity to take an inventory of the young man. Scott Williams was the same height as John but that was where the comparison stopped. He out-weighted John by at least fifty pounds, which appeared to be all muscle. He had a deep, natural tan that she associated with working outdoors every day. Black hair and dark brown eyes, together with a smile that brought out a sexy dimple in his cheek, made him a very attractive young man. She might be getting older but she wasn't blind. *I wonder if he's single or seriously involved with anyone.*

Scott waited until Mary Jones sat down in her chair before he took a seat on the sofa. He sipped his coffee as he studied the older gentleman sitting in the opposite chair. The silver hair was a sure sign that his host had been around a number of years but the blue eyes indicated a highly intelligent man who knew how to listen and analyze information. That was a good thing considering his own agenda and what he hoped would be the outcome of his visit today.

"Have you had a chance to study the property for the best area for the trees?" John got right to the point of the visit. He didn't believe in idle conversation when conducting business. In his experience, people who spent time being too polite and complimentary were less than honest and trying to hide their real motives.

"Yes, the area west of the pond would be the ideal location. The soil samples indicate the perfect mixture of minerals for optimum growth. The natural incline should provide excellent drainage. Based on our earlier telephone conversation, I've prepared an itemized list of the first year's expenses based on a five-acre planting. That includes the cost of the equipment, a storage building, seedlings, and labor costs for the initial planting and the weekly tree maintenance." Scott handed John a file folder.

John read the proposal slowly, asking Scott several questions for clarification. He was impressed with the thoroughness of the report. It was evident that Scott had earned his excellent reputation because he didn't try to oversell the proposal. Scott answered all his questions directly and honestly.

"Can you recommend someone who specializes in the kind of land preparation and maintenance that you've outlined?"

"Actually, I have another proposal for you to consider. I'd like to join Mary and you as a partner in the tree business. I have the equipment needed to prepare the land and experience to plant and maintain the trees. I've attached a list of my educational credentials and several professional and personal references."

After an assessing look at the young man, John stood up and extended his hand to Scott. "Thank you for coming, Scott. You've given us a lot to think about. We're returning to the city tomorrow morning. I'll discuss your proposal with Mary and call you later tonight with an answer."

"It was a pleasure to meet you and I'll look forward to hearing from you." Scott stood up, shook John's hand, thanked Mary for the coffee and walked out the door toward his truck.

"That was an unexpected but interesting turn of events. I'll fix another pot of coffee and a snack tray while you read this prospectus and then we can discuss his proposal." John handed Mary the file folder before walking into the kitchen.

After a lengthy discussion about taking on a partner, John and Mary decided that the advantages out weighted the disadvantages. Having a partner would allow them to explore the many historic landmarks and give them an opportunity to check out the possibility of shipping trees to other parts of the country. They had reached this decision several hours earlier but John hadn't called Scott yet.

Mary studied her husband who was sitting by the fireplace totally absorbed in the book he was reading. "What are you waiting on, John? It's getting late and we have to be up early in the morning to drive back to New York City."

John smiled at the woman who had filled his world with love and laughter for the past thirty years. Long before he had become a successful attorney, she had been his best friend and chief advisor. He closed the book and placed it on the table next to his chair.

"Just a little test, dear. Watching trees grow will take a lot of patience. If Scott Williams can't endure a couple of hours waiting for me to call, then he won't survive the long days of watching trees grow slowly inch by inch. I'll call him before midnight."

CHAPTER ONE

Julie Jones stood looking out the window of her apartment across the street from the campus of Brown University. She could see the old, brick buildings that housed the classrooms and student dorms. In the distance, she could see the bell tower of St. James Methodist Church on Logan Street where she had gone to worship and restore her spirit each week.

The campus sidewalks were covered with students scurrying between the administration hall and the bookstore. It was registration day for incoming freshmen. She knew that they were feeling confused as they tried to absorb all the information being thrown at them and wondering if they would remember half of the directions in the morning.

She was going to miss the quiet beauty of this grand old campus that had been her world for the past six years. The peaceful atmosphere of the library where she had spent so many hours researching term papers was now a part of the past. Last Saturday, she had walked down the aisle to accept her diploma, which had declared to the world that she had graduated with honors, a Masters in Business Management/Public Relations.

Uncle John and Aunt Mary had been there with joy and pride on their faces to help her celebrate that milestone. Even though they weren't her parents, they had given her all the love any child could have ever needed or wanted since she was five years old. Julie knew that, along with the joy, her uncle's heart had been filled with sadness

1

because his brother and sister-in-law weren't there to share their daughter's accomplishments. A tragic plane crash had ended their lives before she had even started elementary school.

It was hard to believe that she had finally completed her education. She had been going to school for the past eighteen years, forever it seemed. Uncle John and Aunt Mary had insisted that she finish her graduate degree before thinking about getting out in the workforce. They were even giving her the opportunity to get some work experience. In two weeks, she would be officially starting her career as the office manager/public relation's officer for the Good Samaritan Tree Farm. This tree farm was her aunt and uncle's pet project to keep them active while they enjoyed their golden years. This would give her the chance to implement her ideas into a successful advertising campaign and give her something to put on her resume.

Julie turned back to survey the apartment she had shared with another graduate student for the last two years. The Early American furnishings in the living room made it a cozy place to relax and study. The kitchen area was little more than a big closet containing a small refrigerator, stove and drop leaf table with two chairs that could be hidden behind louvered doors. There was a laundry area down the hall across from the two tiny bedrooms. The bathroom was so small you barely had room to turn around. As small as the apartment was, it seemed empty today without her roommate's chatter. She was going to miss their late night discussions, which had included everything from the philosophy of life to the latest hunk on campus.

Aimee North's personality was the complete opposite of Julie's but they had become good friends from the first day they met. Julie was a quiet, introvert while Aimee was a talkative, fun loving extrovert. Whenever Julie had become too serious about something, Aimee would start whistling an old cartoon show theme song about a naïve lawman that viewed the world through rose-colored glasses. It had cracked Julie up every time because Aimee wasn't musically inclined. Even when Aimee hummed, the song had been off-key.

Aimee had packed up her belongings and gone home to Vermont yesterday for a short vacation before taking a job at an art museum in New York. Julie had hugged her and promised to keep in touch. They had made plans to get together for lunch at least once a week and an occasional girl's night out.

Julie shook off her melancholy and went back to her packing. There were several boxes stacked at the front door ready to be loaded into her SUV. The only things left to pack were the books and personal items from her desk.

Julie picked up her diploma and read the words printed on the parchment paper. The graduation events of this past week seemed like part of a fantastic dream but this piece of paper was symbolic of all the possibilities that the college president had emphasized in his commencement speech. He'd told them that the future was knocking on their door and they were expected to answer the call enthusiastically. To conquer their fears and go make the world a better place for the next generation. The image his words had created in her mind was so vivid that she could almost hear the rapping of knuckles on wood.

Julie laughed when she realized that the knocking was getting louder and coming from the apartment door. She glanced at her watch and discovered it was time for the new tenants to arrive. Where had the morning gone?

"Just a minute," Julie called out. She placed the diploma on top of the books before opening the door. Standing there was a couple holding hands, oblivious to the hustle and bustle of the other students moving in.

"Please come in," Julie told the couple. "I'm Julie Jones."

"Hello, I'm Bill Lewis and this is my wife, Carol. I hope we're not too early."

"No, your timing is perfect. I just finished packing the last box." Julie assured them. "Why don't you look around while I load these boxes into my vehicle? Then I can answer any questions you might have before I leave."

"Honey, why don't you explore the apartment? I'll help Ms. Jones with these boxes. They're much too heavy for someone your size," he told Julie with a big grin as he flexed his arm muscles.

Julie smiled because she wasn't sure which one of them he was trying to impress. Her or his new wife. "Thank you, I'd appreciate the help. It does my heart good to watch a man work and it will make the loading go faster. I'd like to get on the road as soon as possible. My aunt and uncle worry if I'm on the road after dark."

Bill carried the larger boxes and placed them in the back of the SUV. With the backseat lowered, the cargo space was large enough to hold all the boxes except the two containing her breakable items. She placed these boxes on the passenger side along with her overnight case.

After checking the apartment to make sure she hadn't forgotten anything, she answered a question or two regarding the laundry setup. She handed the keys to the young couple, wished them the best of luck, picked up her purse and walked out the door toward the stairs.

Julie climbed behind the wheel and rolled down the window to let some fresh air inside.

She started the engine and took one last look at the place she had called home. Bill and Carol were standing at the window with their arms around each other. Julie waved goodbye to them and pulled away from the curb.

As she drove along the interstate, it dawned on her that she was getting ready to take on the very real business of living. For the past twenty years, her aunt and uncle had smoothed all the wrinkles in the fabric of her life but now it was time to leave the schoolgirl behind and become an adult. The office manager slash/relations job would allow her to prove that she had could contribute to the success of a business in the real world not just outline the steps in a term paper.

Will this new life include a husband and children? Someone to share the dreams, the laughter and tears with each day?

She had dated during college, but there hadn't been anyone special lately. Her one attempt at a serious relationship hadn't been that successful. She and Steve Green had attended the same English Literature class during her freshman year. The attraction had been mutual. After dating for a couple of months, they had moved in together eager to experience the sexual revolution for themselves. It hadn't lasted very long.

Julie wasn't sure exactly how it had happened but the complication of going to classes, studying for test, and the reality of daily living had soon made them rethink their relationship. They came to the conclusion that it would be easier to endure the demands of college life if they were not living together. They both agreed that there was more to an adult relationship than having someone to hold during the night, that they didn't really have the same goals in life. They had remained close friends until he graduated two years ago. Since then she hadn't really bothered with dating much. She had decided to concentrate her energy on her classes and the various clubs she had joined. Besides, she wasn't sure if there was a man who could meet the image she had in her head and in her heart.

Aimee and she had sorted the guys on campus into two categories: the athletic jocks, who were only serious about sports and the eggheads, who would forget they had a date with you if they were involved in a project. The ones in the first category had been physically attractive and fun to be with but their conversations centered around their latest accomplishments, while those in the second category were able to discuss world events intelligently but they seemed a little on the wimpy side. In her mind, the perfect man would be a combination of both types.

He would be tender and loving toward women and children but still be able to change a tire without fear of ruining his hands. A man who would command the respect of his friends by his dedication to the things he believed to be important. She wanted the kind of love she had witnessed between her aunt and uncle as she had grown up. She wanted a man to look at her with that same kind of love in his eyes and know, without a doubt, that she was the only person who could make his world complete. And vice versa.

CHAPTER TWO

The early morning was quiet with only the occasional chatter of squirrels to interrupt his thoughts as Scott Williams looked out the window of his kitchen. He watched as the sun began to appear, gilding the oak leaves and making them appear a deeper shade of red. He always got a feeling of peace and contentment at sunrise. He knew that the sun would do its job of warming the earth to make all of nature's miracles like grass, flowers, and trees grow. In his line of work that was very important. As he looked out over the seemingly endless rows of fir trees that stretched to the horizon and beyond to the edge of the tree farm, he recalled his meeting with the Joneses and how all this had begun.

Why didn't they call? Scott had been asking himself that question all evening. Waiting on John Jones to call had made this the longest day of his entire life. He really wanted this partnership because it would let him work outdoors, planting and growing trees.

When the Joneses had first contacted him about an evaluation of their property with their intention of turning it into a tree farm, he had approached it like any other consulting job. But as he had worked up the proposal, it occurred to him that they would need someone to take care of the physical labor involved, given their age. It had seemed like the perfect opportunity for him to realize one part of his dreams for the future. To start a business of his own, doing what he loved best.

For the past two hours, he had alternated between trying to read, glancing at the clock on the wall and pacing the room. So far, he had read the same page five times without remembering a single word and almost worn a hole in the carpet. From the way he had been pacing, you'd think he was an expectant father who was too nervous to sit still.

Scott poured another cup of coffee and returned to the book he had been attempting to read but he couldn't seem to focus his mind. He counted the chimes as the mantle clock declared the hour. Eleven o'clock. John Jones hadn't seemed like a man who wouldn't keep his word but it looked like he wasn't going to call tonight. Scott couldn't help feeling a rush of disappointment. He had been sure that the timing was right.

Scott was turning out the lights before going to bed when the phone finally rang. The first ring had barely had time to end before he grabbed the receiver. His heart was pounding so hard he could barely breathe. "Hello."

"Scott, John Jones here. Mary and I have been discussing your proposal and we'd like to take you up on your partnership offer. Can you come into New York City tomorrow afternoon? We can sign a partnership contract and get a business account established. You'll need cash for the expenses of getting the tree farm started." The only thing John heard from the receiver was silence. He waited a minute. "Are you still there, Scott?"

"Yes, I'm here. I'll be in New York by one o'clock." Scott could hardly believe that he was getting the chance to start his own business. Not exactly his alone but he remembered something his father had said...Dream big but start small. It had worked for his father. By the time Thomas Williams had retired, he had expanded a small art supply shop into a chain of stores all over the New England area.

Scott walked out onto the deck of the cabin he had built last year when he'd needed to spend more and more hours tending the trees. The cabin was located a quarter mile from the Jones house. John and Mary had offered him the use of their home when he had first talked about needing to live on the property, but he hadn't wanted to deprive them of their country retreat. He knew how much they liked getting away from the city occasionally. Besides, he enjoyed their visits. It gave him the chance to show them how the trees were progressing instead of just reporting by phone or email.

The computer he had purchased last year had made it much easier to keep in touch with them and his mom loved it. She emailed him every week to see how he was doing and his sister emailed him to brag about his two nephew's baseball prowess or send the latest family pictures. His nephews were growing up so fast. Whenever he looked at the pictures, it made him eager to start a family of his own. Scott wanted his own bragging rights.

Scott realized that he wasn't getting any younger. If he didn't get started soon, he would be too old to do all the things a father and son enjoyed doing together. But that would have to wait until the tree farm was on solid ground financially. It wouldn't be fair to ask a woman to share the hardships of a fledgling business. His plan was to give the business two years to develop a clientele, show a profit. Then if everything went well he'd start looking for a wife.

He wanted to meet a woman who could love him and share a home with him and a couple of kids. Six years of long, hard days working on the farm hadn't left much time for the usual bachelor's social life. His evenings had been solitary ones except for an occasional poker game with some of the guys in town. It was an excellent plan but right now he had to concentrate on making the first part a success.

This would be the first season of sales for Good Samaritan Tree Farm. The tree farm represented John and Mary's dream of donating trees to orphanages and nursing homes for the holidays. It made him sad to think about the forgotten senior citizens and all the unwanted boys and girls in the world. He couldn't wait to see the looks on the children's faces when they arrived with a tree for them to help decorate, especially the youngest ones who didn't have many happy memories. Christmas should be a magical time for children.

As he walked along surveying the trees, he couldn't help the feelings of pride and accomplishment that he felt. The fruits of his labor were clearly visible. The donation trees were the best he had ever seen. Because he considered them a special labor of love, he'd spent extra time shaping the trees to make them as perfect as possible.

9

Scott had reached the access road that intersected the sections of trees when he noticed some unusual footprints mixed in with the tracks of the various animals that had passed through during the night. He bent down to examine the ground. The indentions were small and would appear to have been made by sneakers. That meant the footprints had been made by kids. He'd phone John when he got back to the cabin and see if they had brought any visitors with them yesterday. He had been in town buying supplies and had missed them by a few minutes. He didn't want someone wandering around the property without getting permission.

It was noon by the time Scott inspected the last section of trees and started back to his cabin for lunch. He stopped to look at the sign Mary had designed and painted for the entry gateway. It was a mural that depicted a family picking out a Christmas tree to chop down while another little boy and girl helped their father tie a tree on the luggage rack of a car. It was reminiscent of a *Norman Rockwell* painting of simpler times. A time when families enjoyed doing things together, instead of parents scurrying around to get each child to all the activities that they participated in each day and getting ulcers in the process.

The sign reminded him that simple pleasures were what made life worthwhile. Simple things like visiting with the good friends he had made since moving into his cabin. The local sheriff was a classmate from high school who had recommended him to John and Mary Jones.

Scott really enjoyed the small town atmosphere of Spencer City. When he went into town to get supplies, the storeowners all knew him by name. The older ladies in town would bake him cookies and casseroles. They even tried to fix him up with a girlfriend occasionally. They might seem a little nosy at times, but he knew that the townspeople truly cared about whether he was happy or sad. He knew he could call on them for help and they would drop everything and come immediately.

As he stepped up on the deck of the cabin, Scott could hear the phone ringing. He hurried inside to check the caller ID before answering. It read J&M Jones. "Hello, you're just the person I wanted to talk to."

"Hello, yourself," an amused feminine voice replied. The underlying laughter he heard in her voice made his lips quiver in response. It was definitely not Mary's voice. This voice had a slightly husky lilt to it that made his pulse race.

"This is Julie Jones, John and Mary's niece. They've hired me to manage the business end of the tree farm. I'd like to discuss the goals of the business and get a feel for possible advertising angles. Are you free for dinner tomorrow evening?"

"Yes, I'm free. What time is dinner?" Scott sounded abrupt but his brain was having trouble functioning.

"Drinks are at seven o'clock. My aunt and uncle have told me a lot of nice things about you. I'm looking forward to meeting you and working with you this fall."

"I'll see you tomorrow night. Tell Mary I'll bring a bottle of her favorite wine."

Scott stood holding the telephone receiver and staring into space long after the line went dead. His mind was replaying the short conversation with Julie Jones. The words she'd spoken weren't anything special but his heart was racing in reaction to the mere sound of a woman's voice. Scott smiled at the images that her sexy voice had created in his mind. Dining by candlelight, slow dancing, making love on a moonlit beach until the rising sun appeared out of the waves. *Good grief! Those kinds of thoughts were for sentimental fools.*

His body tightened with desire as all these scenarios chased one another through his mind. Scott couldn't remember the last time he had been on a date with an attractive woman much less anything more intimate. His reaction to this unseen woman was a sure sign that he really needed to get out more socially. He walked into the kitchen, opened the refrigerator and took out some cold cuts and bread. He fixed himself a sandwich, opened a bag of chips and sat down at the table to eat. It was probably just hunger that was causing such a crazy reaction to a woman's voice on the phone. But in his mind he knew better. His body knew exactly what it needed and it wasn't food.

Scott tried to recall what he knew about the woman he had just spoken to on the phone.

11

Julie had grown up in New York City as a member of one of the wealthiest families in New England. She was a graduate of a prestigious college, a career woman who was eager to make a place for herself in the business world. There were probably dozens of men in the city falling over each other to ask her out on dates, to take her to Broadway shows and fancy restaurants.

A woman like that wouldn't be interested in a man who loved the quiet country life. A man who thought an ideal date was spending a quiet evening at home not clubbing in the city. A man like him.

After placing the call to Scott, Julie had a hard time concentrating on writing thank you notes for the graduation gifts she had received from her friends. Scott's deep masculine voice had a soft, low resonance to it that sent shivers sliding up her spine. Julie couldn't help wondering what it would be like to hear that voice whispering in her ear late at night. To hear him describe all the sensual things she wanted him to do.

She was putting a stamp on the last envelope when she had a sudden urge to talk to her old roommate. She pickup up the phone and dialed the number for the art museum where Aimee worked as Assistant Curator.

"Up-Town Museum, Ms. North." The voice sounded too professional to be happy-go-lucky Aimee.

"This is Julie Jones. I have one question. Who are you and want have you done with the real Aimee."

"Cut it out, Jones," Aimee told her. "I'm trying to sound worthy of this fancy title."

"If you haven't had lunch, why don't you meet me at Mario's in thirty minutes? I need answers to some man questions," Julie told her old friend and confidant.

"Don't tell me that the Great Fortress has been breeched at last by some lucky Knight. What's his name? Is it someone I know? I want all the juicy details." Aimee exclaimed in an exaggerated lecherous voice.

"How can I tell you anything when you won't let me get a word in edgewise? Here are the answers to your questions. No lucky knight. The drawbridge is still securely fastened against an invasion. You don't know him but his name is Scott Williams. He's a partner with Uncle John and Aunt Mary in the tree farm business that they began the year we started college. I just spoke to the man on the phone and his voice sounded very...nice. I'll be working closely with him for the next three months and wanted to get your advice on how to approach the situation. I've got a gut feeling that I'll need all your expertise in this area. Especially if Scott looks half as good as he sounds."

"Can I interpret the phrase 'very nice' to mean sexy?"

"Oh, yeah. Extremely."

"Well, you've come to the right place. I'll meet you at Mario's. I'll be the one with the expression of wisdom on her face. Dear Aimee's hourly rates are real cheap. One hour/one fir tree," Aimee teased her friend but in her heart she wanted to shout with exhilaration.

Aimee had set her up with some to the hottest guys on campus during their two years in grad school but none of them had clicked. Julie was such a wonderful person. She deserved to find someone to love, someone who would treasure her beautiful spirit.

"You've got yourself a deal. One tree for one hour of counseling." Julie replied.

CHAPTER THREE

Rush hour traffic was running at its usual frantic pace as Scott drove into downtown New York City. Bumper to bumper traffic along with the name calling from the drivers reminded him of why he preferred the slower pace of Spencer City to the constant activity of a large city.

The streets were crowded with thousands of people trying to get home from work and the early shoppers hoping to get ahead of the crowds as they looked for Christmas gifts. There were others, who had driven in from the suburbs to go to the theatre, have dinner with friends, or simply to watch the lights being put on the tree in Rockefeller Plaza, a tradition that had been going on for more than seventy years. The congestion reminded him of salmon trying to battle the rapids as they swam upstream.

Scott spotted an empty parking space just ahead. He parked his truck and started walking toward the square. The wine he wanted to buy was in a little shop a couple of blocks away. Walking would give him a chance to work off some of his nervous energy. He had been pre-occupied all day with thoughts of the dinner that lay ahead. To be honest, his thoughts were about the woman he was going to meet.

Street vendors were doing a booming business tonight as people stopped to buy hotdogs, cups of hot coffee and bags of chestnuts to eat while they watched the workers placing strings of lights on the humungous tree. There must be at least a million tiny lights. The official lighting ceremony was scheduled for next week.

Beyond the tree, he could see dozens of ice skaters enjoying the rink below. He stopped to watch them for a few minutes. One girl was weaving in and out among the other skaters without missing a single step. He watched her execute a triple jump that was good enough for the Olympics. Scott was getting ready to leave when he noticed the older couple.

They were slowly circling the rink, skating in perfect unison, holding hands and talking quietly to each other. They seemed to be totally unaware of the other skaters moving around them. The woman was listening intently to what the man was saying with such a loving expression on her face and the gentleman was smiling back at her with the same look of blissful happiness in his eyes. It was as if they were the only people on the ice or in the world. The beauty of that look made him swallow the sudden lump he got in his throat. It must be nice to know you were the center of someone's world.

Everywhere he looked he saw couples laughing with each other. He was beginning to think that everybody had someone except him. He turned and continued walking down the street toward Venetti Wines.

He entered the wine shop and looked around at the holiday decorations. Santa Claus and his sleigh, complete with all eight reindeer, were sitting on a shelf over the doorway into the stockroom. Rudolph's nose was a flashing red bulb. Several green-clad elves were standing on each other's shoulders loading the sleigh with presents that the other elves were passing along in fire brigade fashion. He could hear someone singing along with an operatic aria playing on a radio. It was nice to know that some things never changed.

It didn't take him long to find the wine he wanted because the store layout hadn't been changed in the ten years he had been buying wine. It was Angelo Venetti's theory that people didn't want to take time from their busy schedules to hunt for wine when they stopped by his shop. They were in too much of a hurry these days. They didn't take any time to enjoy the art of choosing a wine. The old man must be wise to the ways of the customers because his business had been thriving for years. Scott approached the register and set the bottle of wine down to be rung up.

"Good evening, Mr. Venetti. How are you feeling today?" he asked the elderly man standing behind the counter.

"I'm just fine." He shook hands with the young man. "I haven't seen you in the store for quite a while. Where have you been keeping yourself?"

"The tree farm has kept me pretty busy lately. The holiday season is almost here and I've spent most of my time getting the trees ready for market. We'll be having a grand opening soon. Why don't you bring Mrs. Venetti out that weekend and pick out a nice tree to put in the shop? A beautifully decorated tree would look very festive in the corner by the front window and catch the eye of the shopper's as they pass the shop."

"That's a good idea. I'll talk to my Anna and see what she thinks." He walked over to the back of the shop and yelled up the stairway. "Anna, come down and say hello to our guest."

Scott could hear the lady in question muttering to herself in Italian about the manners of a certain gentleman. He laughed as Mr. Venetti shrugged his shoulders to indicate his opinion of her complaints about him.

He watched as the petite, dark-haired lady entered the shop with surprising speed when he considered she was not young anymore. She threw up her hands in surprise and rushed over to give him a big hug and kiss. Mrs. Venetti had been treating him like one of the family ever since he had come home with their son, Dominic, one weekend from college.

"It is so good to see you, bambino. You must stay and eat with us. The sauce is almost ready and there is a big bowl of pasta just waiting to be eaten. You know I always make plenty just in case Maria or Dominic decide to drop by."

"Can I have a rain check on that pasta? I'm dining with friends tonight and just stopped by to get a special bottle of wine to take to the hostess."

"Of course, you are welcome anytime. If you ever find yourself a girl, you can bring her as well," Mr. Venetti told him with a twinkle in his eye.

Scott paid for the wine and waved goodbye to the shopkeeper and his wife as he went out the door. Since it was still too early for dinner, he sat down on a bench in front of the shop to absorb the ambiance of the holiday scene.

The sidewalks were a mass of bodies as the shoppers hurried from one shop to another.

As he looked around, he wondered if the people passing by remembered the real purpose of gift giving. Were they so busy trying to find the perfect present that they didn't stop to consider what that person really wanted? Or were they just trying to make a good impression on a certain person? An expensive gift wasn't worth a nickel if it was only given out of obligation or duty.

When it came to gift giving during the holiday season, love was a necessary ingredient and made all the difference in the world.

Scott noticed a young man and woman as they stopped nearby to look in the window of a lingerie shop. The mannequins were decked out in a variety of sleepwear. From thermal underwear to footed pajamas that guaranteed the wearer would be snug and warm for the cold winter nights. Then there were the more provocative peignoirs. Sheer, lacy items that were intended to make their bed partner's temperature high enough to keep them both warm throughout the night.

He couldn't help but overhear the couple as they carried on a lively discussion about the merits of one sleepwear over another. The man seemed to think the lace teddy was nice but the woman was pointing out that a pair of flannel pajamas would be more practical since they would keep her warm. The man put his arm around her waist, pulled her up close to him and whispered something in her ear. The woman laughed and poked him playfully in the ribs before giving him a look that promised special attention later.

A sudden longing for someone to laugh with made Scott realize what was missing from his life. A soul mate that could make the world seem like a magical place. He had some good friends but not that special woman to share his life with or to enjoy the simple act of shopping for gifts during the Christmas season. Instantly, he recalled a woman's voice on the phone.

A glance at his watch showed him that it was almost seven o'clock. He drove the short distance to 6th Street where the Joneses lived and parked the truck. Scott sat there for a moment trying to get his thoughts organized. He wanted Julie's first impression of him to be a good one. He didn't want it to be of a man who couldn't even talk without sounding like a babbling idiot.

He'd been trying to imagine what kind of personality Julie would have. Would she be one of those women's lib types who were self-centered and obnoxious or would she be like her aunt who was a very self-confident woman. Mary knew how to make everyone feel at ease without lessening her own importance. Since Julie and he were going to be seeing each other daily, it would be nice if they could at least develop a good working relationship.

When he'd signed the partnership papers six years ago, he'd seen a picture on John's desk of a young freckled-faced girl on horseback with her hair in pigtails. In all these years, he and Julie had never actually met. She was either at school or out with friends when he'd visited John and Mary. *What would she look like today as a young woman?* Scott asked himself.

He had been fantasizing about her all day. He told himself that it was because she was a woman he would have to work closely with for the next three months. A woman whose voice had occupied his dreams all night. Dreams that had made it necessary to take a cold shower this morning to stop his blood from strumming through his veins at a feverish pace.

Maybe, she would have big, rabbit teeth and thick glasses then he wouldn't have to worry about being attracted to her. That just might work. He'd be okay as long as he didn't hear her speak in that sultry voice that he couldn't seem to get out of his head.

Scott locked the truck, walked to the townhouse door and took a deep breath before he rang the doorbell. He hadn't been this agitated since he'd gone on his first date when he was fifteen. *I don't understand why I'm so nervous. My hands are sweaty. My heart's pumping so fast it's making me dizzy. I don't usually have this much anxiety when meeting new people.*

* * * * *

The man pacing up and down in front of the deserted warehouse on the dock had pulled his black Fedora down low to meet the turned up collar of his cashmere trench coat. The only streetlight was at the corner of the warehouse but he wasn't taking any chance of being recognized. He was meeting a man to solicit his special services, a man who would determine the outcome of his whole future. The waiting was making him antsy. He looked at his gold Rolex watch to make sure it was still working. Five minutes to go.

A dark sedan stopped within five feet of him and an average looking man dressed in a wrinkled raincoat opened the car door. He got out and slowly scanned the area for any activity that was out of the ordinary or suspicious. Satisfied that they were the only people on the dock, he approached the other man. "Did you bring the fee we discussed?"

"Yes, I brought the money." The first man handed over a duffel bag. "Inside you'll find the PI report and information you'll need including a recent picture. There's a contact number to call when the job is over or if you run into problems. Leave a number and message time. Add 911 if you need a quick answer. I'll be checking that number daily and I'll call you back."

The two men shook hands and went their separate ways quickly to make sure nobody could link them together. Each man was trying to analyze the meeting and the ultimate outcome. Neither one noticed that the pile of rags in the shadow of the dumpster was actually a homeless man who had overheard every word of their conversation.

CHAPTER FOUR

John was in the den getting bottles of liquor out that he'd need for mixing the drinks. Mary was busy adding the finishing touches to the dinner preparations and Julie was arranging hors d' oeuvres on a tray when the doorbell rang.

"Julie, can you get the door? I'll join you as soon as I put this casserole in the oven to melt the cheese topping."

"Sure." Julie wiped her hands on a towel and walked down the hallway.

She'd spent the whole day listening to her aunt praise Scott's attributes. According to her, Scott was a cross between Superman and a heavenly angel. While they'd been getting the dinner preparations started this afternoon, Aunt Mary had been dropping hints about how nice Scott was and that it was a shame he was still single at thirty years old. Aunt Mary had even confided her plan to lure him into the city for a New Year's Eve party and introduce Scott to the daughters of her bridge club friends. Maybe she should warn the poor man that her aunt was going to play matchmaker.

When Julie opened the door, she was pleasantly surprised to discover that Scott Williams was just as ruggedly handsome as her aunt had implied. The man didn't look like the type who would need help from anyone when it came to finding a date. The female species had probably been chasing him since junior high.

She had to admit that he was impressive, though. Julie let her eyes wander over his physique for a quick inventory of his assets. He was an inch or two over six foot and his broad shoulders filled out his corduroy jacket quite nicely. Long, muscular legs were encased in denim jeans. A tanned face with dark brown eyes, framed by incredibly long eyelashes, went perfectly with the black hair that was curling against the collar of his jacket. Her first thought was that he was a very handsome man. But then he smiled and she changed that adjective to gorgeous. That smile showed off his dimples plus a twinkle in his eyes that took her breath away and made rational thinking difficult. The man clearly should be labeled hazardous to all females, from babies to grandmothers. She cleared her throat and tried to focus her thoughts as she extended her hand.

"Hello, I'm Julie. You must be Scott."

"Yes, I am. It's nice to meet you, Julie." Scott took her hand in his. He stood there looking into the most beautiful eyes he had ever seen. They were the color of emeralds and shining as brightly as the stars in the sky. Sable brown hair hung down past her shoulders in soft waves. He wanted to run his fingers through the curls to see if they were as soft and silky as they looked. The girl with pigtails and freckles was gone. She had turned into the beautiful, vibrant woman standing in front of him.

"Please come in. Uncle John's in the den mixing drinks." Julie glanced down at their hands, which were still clasped. The contact was making her whole arm tingle. It was a reaction she had never experienced before. She slowly removed her hand and walked down the hallway to the den.

Scott closed the door and followed Julie down the hallway. From this vantage point, he couldn't help but notice that her figure was just as perfect as her face. She was slender but not supermodel thin and blessed with curves in all the right places. Tall enough to place her head on his shoulder if they were slow dancing. Thinking about her body snuggling up to him and watching the gentle sway of her hips as she walked had his body reacting like any normal red-blooded male. He quickly buttoned his jacket to hide the fact that a certain part of his body was making his slacks uncomfortably tight.

As they approached the doorway into the den, Mary came out of the kitchen carrying the tray of hors d'oeuvres. She walked ahead of them into the den and placed the tray on the coffee table. Scott kissed Mary on the cheek and gave her a quick hug, then crossed over to the bar and shook hands with John.

"What would you like to drink, Scott?" John asked.

"Scotch, neat." Scott hoped the fiery liquid would help combat the heat of his libido.

"I'll be right back as soon as I put this wine in the refrigerator to chill."

Scott quickly left the den and entered the kitchen. Opening the refrigerator, he placed the wine on a shelf. He leaned his head against the cool surface of the refrigerator door and took a deep breath. He needed a minute to let his body recover and get his breathing back to normal.

He hadn't had such an intense response to a female since junior high school when his newly awakened hormones were on 24/7 alert and Jill Jackson had returned from summer vacation with a drastic increase in her bra cup size. He had found the change fascinating.

His reaction to Julie had him a little confused because he was afraid that these feelings were more than just sexual attraction. He had never believed in love at first sight but one look into Julie's green eyes and he could have sworn he heard bells ringing. *Get a grip! You're a grown man not some lovesick teenager!* Taking another deep breath, he went back into the den.

"Here's your drink." As Scott approached the bar that occupied one corner of the room, John handed him the glass and together they walked over to the seating area.

Twin leather couches faced each other in front of an Italian marble fireplace. Mary and Julie were seated on one couch arranging the plates and napkins on the table that was placed between the couches. Scott helped himself to a cracker piled high with pate before sitting down across from the women. He wanted to be able to observe Julie as they talked.

"Julie, I'd like to formally introduce you to our friend and partner, Scott Williams. Scott, this is our niece, Julie Jones. She'll be doing the accounting and publicity for the tree farm." Mary smiled with obvious pride at the young woman seated next to her.

"Hello, again. I don't have any first hand experience in the tree farm business so I'll need to consult with you about the practical nature of growing trees. Then I'll have a better idea of the best direction to take on the advertising angles." She had the same no-nonsense approach to business as her uncle. "I know why Uncle John and Aunt Mary wanted to start the tree farm but I'd like to know why you wanted to be their partner?"

"Ever since I was a young boy, I've enjoyed exploring the forest near our home. Because I wanted to work outdoors, I decided to major in Forestry Preservation in college. I worked for the State Forestry Commission for the first two years after college but I felt that I could be doing more to improve the environment. When your aunt and uncle contacted me requesting a land evaluation, I saw an opportunity to realize the dream of having my own business."

Scott took a sip of Scotch as he tried to think of a way to state his philosophy of life without sounding like a Pollyanna.

"I really liked the idea of bringing the Christmas spirit of love to unwanted children who have so little joy in their lives. Children shouldn't have to face the harsh realities of the world until they've had the chance to enjoy being a child. If we can give just a few happy memories then all the hard work will be worth it.

I'm looking forward to seeing the look of wonder in their eyes when they open their presents. Seeing their excitement will bring back my own memories of Christmas mornings with my family. I remember being so excited on Christmas Eve that I had a hard time going to sleep. I even imagined that I held the reindeer prancing on the roof. You know what they say. A boy never grows up when it comes to the holidays. That the toys just get more expensive." Scott's grin made the dimples appear in his checks.

Julie's could just see a younger version of this man waking everyone up at the crack of dawn to see what Santa had brought him. Her heart swelled with emotion and her face was lit by a secret smile.

"A few of my friends thought it was foolish to take such a big risk, but I haven't regretted my decision to join John and Mary. Even if the tree farm doesn't make me a rich man, I will consider it successful because I will have acquired two very good friends." Scott took another sip of his drink and waited for the next question.

In the silence that followed, he glanced at Julie and found her looking at him with an amazed expression on her face.

Mary looked at John and lifted an eyebrow when she observed Julie's reaction to the sincerity in Scott's voice. They both smiled at this development.

When Julie noticed them looking at her in amusement, she blushed and went to put her wine glass on the bar. She didn't want to give her aunt more ammunition for her matchmaking scheme. From the kitchen, a buzzer sounded. Her aunt rose from the couch and started out the doorway. As she left the den, Mary announced that dinner would be ready in five minutes.

Julie watched as John and Scott stood up and approached the bar. They were both such handsome men. Her uncle with his silvered hair was the epitome of a sophisticated man who was confident in his ability to navigate the legal morass of the courts. Scott, on the other hand, looked like a man who could handle any obstacle that the world handed him single-handedly. Battle the elements of nature until he tamed them. Those muscles hadn't come from a gym but from physical labor and working outdoors had given him a natural tan that made him look good enough to be on the cover of any outdoorsman's magazine.

"If you'll excuse me, I'll help Aunt Mary get the food on the table." Julie told them. She needed to put some distance between Scott and herself to counteract the strong physical response she felt. A response that she'd never experienced before. He seemed to have a heart as big as the outdoors he loved so much. When Scott had described his feelings about Christmas and presents for kids, she had found herself wanting to caress his cheek and offer to help plant those trees.

Dinner was served in the elegant dining room that included an impressive chandelier and a mahogany table covered by a white damask tablecloth and matching napkins. The floral centerpiece was a mixture of fall flowers and silk vegetables. Waterford crystal, Wedgwood china and gold-plated eating utensils completed the table settings.

Julie looked up directly into the eyes of the man who had been occupying most of her thoughts even as she had added her suggestions for the ad campaign. She knew that the food her aunt had prepared was delicious but she had barely touched it. Mostly, she was rearranging it on her dinner plate. She had only taken a few bites to make it appear that she was eating. Julie had never had any attraction affect her appetite.

All during dinner, Scott's eyes had constantly wandered to the lovely girl sitting across the table. The lights from the chandelier brought out the red highlights in Julie's hair. He was having a difficult time concentrating on the conversation that was going on at the table. They were discussing the various ways to advertise the tree farm. He could hear them speaking but he didn't have a clue about what they were actually saying.

"Scott, which day do you think would be best for the grand opening?" When there wasn't any response, John repeated his name. "Scott?"

John's voice startled Scott out of his daydreaming. "I'm sorry. What did you say? I was trying to remember something that I needed to ask you. I must be getting old. I can't keep two thoughts in my head at the same time."

"I asked if you had a date in mind for the grand opening." With an amused grin, John saw a slight blush appear on Scott's face. He'd seen him staring at Julie and had a pretty good idea what thoughts were going on in Scott's head. He wasn't so old that he couldn't remember the way a beautiful woman could derail a man's mind.

"The last weekend in November would be the best time, I think. Some people like to put their trees up right after the Thanksgiving holiday. The trees still need a little shaping but I can have that finished in two weeks."

Scott picked up his glass to take a sip of his wine. He glanced over the rim of his glass at the woman sitting across the table. At that exact moment, Julie flicked a drop of wine off her lips with her tongue before it could dribble down her chin. That simple action made him take a gulp instead of a sip of his own wine. The liquid went down the wrong way and caused him to go into a coughing jag to keep from choking. John came around the table to slap him on the back several times.

"Are you okay?" Mary asked him.

"Yes, I'm fine.' Scott picked up his water glass and took a small sip to soothe his throat. "Evidently, drinking and talking doesn't mix any better than drinking and driving. I think I'll stick to water for the rest of the meal."

"Two weeks should give me plenty of time to get the advertising plans organized and implemented, as well." Julie told them. She found Scott's enthusiasm for the tree farm and the special project for public service contagious. She couldn't wait to share her ideas with him. Of course, it didn't hurt that he was attractive. She only hoped that she could keep her mind on advertising.

"Julie, why don't you stay in our house at the tree farm?" Mary asked her niece. "You can use the extra guest room as an office. We can get any office equipment that you'll need in the morning and take it over to Spencer City tomorrow afternoon. The sooner you get started on the ad campaign the better."

"That's a good idea. You'll be closer to the local towns for the advertising and you won't have to commute back and forth," John agreed with lots of enthusiasm. "I'd feel a lot better knowing you aren't driving that distance everyday."

"Okay. I'll move my things tomorrow," Julie agreed with a suspicious look at her aunt and uncle. What were those two up to? Their wide-eyed looks of innocent were a sure sign of mischief.

"Then it's all settled," Mary told them. "I think that's enough business talk for one evening. Let's have our dessert in the den. Julie, will you carry the coffee for me?"

As Scott and John walked down the hall toward the den, he suddenly remembered the footprints. "I'm sorry I missed you yesterday. Did you bring anyone else out with you when you came by the farm?"

"No, it was just Mary and I. Why?" John replied quickly. "Is there a problem?"

"I noticed some footprints that must have been made by small children. Probably just kids using the road as a shortcut. I'll let you know if I notice anything else unusual."

Mary and Julie came into the den a few minutes later with two trays. One tray held a silver coffee service and the other had individual ramekins filled with cheesecake topped with fresh berries. Julie served the cheesecake while Mary poured the coffee.

Scott took a bite of his cheesecake and gave a murmur of pleasure as he tasted the richness of the delicate dessert. The texture of the filling was incredible smooth while the berries had a distinct flavor that he couldn't quite place.

"Mary, this cheesecake is wonderful. It's the best I've ever eaten. Did you bake it yourself or did it come from one of the local bakeries?" Scott asked between bites.

"Actually, Julie baked them from her own special recipe. She's always had a knack for adding some little something to make desserts extraordinary. She inherited that talent from her mother, who was a gourmet chef. We've always been amazed that she could combine brains, beauty and be such a good cook. So many of the young women today only know how to microwave foods or order takeout."

"Aunt Mary's exaggerating and I think we can assume that she is a little biased." Julie gave her aunt a loving glance. "I just happen to enjoy puttering around in the kitchen. Anybody who can read a cookbook can learn to cook. It's a matter of trial and error."

"Whatever the rationale, you can make this cheesecake anytime you want to please the junior boss in this business." Scott's eyes had a gleam in them that suggested he wasn't just thinking about food.

"I'll keep that in mind for when I make a total mess of the bookkeeping files."

After finishing dessert and coffee, Scott reluctantly announced that it was time he got back to the farm. He wasn't ready for the evening to end, but at least he knew he would be seeing Julie tomorrow. With her living next door, he could get to know her better. After all, business decisions would need to be discussed regularly.

"Thanks for the excellent meal, Mary." Scott stood up, shook hands with John and wished the ladies good night. "I'll see everyone tomorrow afternoon."

"I'll see Scott out and lock up." Julie told her aunt and uncle. She followed Scott out of the den. Because her back was to them, she didn't see the triumphant smiles or high fives that John and Mary gave each other.

Scott opened the door and turned to wish Julie goodnight. The streetlights shining in the doorway casts a soft glow making her facial features appear ethereal. She was so beautiful standing there smiling at him that he had difficulty speaking because the urge to take her into

28

his arms was so strong. He took a step back and extended his hand toward Julie.

"Welcome to the business. I wasn't sure how taking on a manager would work out but after meeting you I believe it's going to be the best thing for everyone. The future is looking brighter already."

"Thank you. It was nice to meet you, too. I look forward to working with you. I'll do my best to not let anyone down." Julie placed her hand in his. The skin was a little rough but the warmth of his palm sent a shiver down her spine. Her eyes followed him as he walked down the steps to the sidewalk and opened the door of his truck.

"Goodnight, Scott. Be careful driving home." Scott raised a hand in farewell and drove down the street. Julie watched until the taillights of his truck disappeared around the corner before closing the door.

She went down the hall and opened the kitchen door. John and Mary were putting the leftovers in the fridge and loading the dishwasher. "If you don't mind, I'll go get my things together for the trip tomorrow."

As Julie removed her clothes from the dresser and repacked her suitcases, she was glad that she hadn't gotten around to unpacking everything. Most of the boxes were still in the SUV. She wasn't getting much packing done because she kept thinking about Scott. He was making her rethink her preconceived notions about men. He looked like a football linebacker, but he was so gentle and caring. Any woman lucky enough to be loved by him would feel protected and treasured at the same time.

She shook her head and told herself that she needed to concentrate on the job instead of mooning over the first attractive man that she met. When she remembered the twinkle in those gorgeous brown eyes, she sighed deeply because her hormones were running amuck after only one encounter. This was the absolute worst time to develop an attraction. Why did it have to be Scott that stirred all these feeling in her?

It was going to be an impossible to avoid him when they would be practically living in each other's pocket for the next three months. Seeing him everyday was going to be a severe strain on her nerves. She'd have to be constantly on guard when she was around him, to try to limit the time that they spent alone so she wouldn't be tempted. Heaven help her if the man ever decided to seduce her because she knew in her heart that she wouldn't be able to resist.

Maybe she'd write and ask Santa to bring her a special present this year for Christmas. A little something that would fit in a small, square box with a fancy bow. She would prefer an expensive piece of jewelry with enough diamonds to make all this self-imposed sacrifice bearable. *Scott would look real good under the tree with just a smile and a red bow placed strategically.*

Scott found himself humming along with the radio station as he drove back to Spencer City. Happiness seemed to be bubbling up from deep inside him and it needed an outlet. The uncontrollable urge to laugh, sing or shout was making him smile from ear to ear. He wanted to stop the truck, get out and declare to the heavens that the woman he'd been searching for had been found. He needed to tell someone to make it seem real.

The sudden ringing of his cell phone startled him out of his daydreaming. It took a minute for him to remove it from his jacket pocket and push the answer button. "Hello."

"Hi, little brother. It's Diana. I'm up with a sick boy and I thought I'd see how you've been doing. I figured I'd have to wake you up."

"It's a good thing I wasn't asleep. You could have given me a heart attack. A telephone call at this hour is usually bad news." Scott told her in an exasperated voice. "But I'm glad you called. I was just wishing that I could talk to someone."

"Why? Is something wrong?"

The concern in he heard in Diana's voice reminded him that she had always tried to fix all his scrapes and bruises when they were growing up.

"No. As a matter of fact, everything is wonderful. My health is excellent. The tree farm will be opening for business next month and tonight I met a wife."

"You did what? Scott, have you been drinking. You sound like you're either drunk or high."

"Well, I did have wine with dinner but I'm in complete control of my faculties. The high you hear in my voice is the exuberance of falling in love."

"Really. Where did you meet this woman? Is she from Spencer City? I didn't think you ever left the farm. Tell me more."

"I met Julie at John and Mary Joneses house. She's their niece and tomorrow she will be from Spencer City. Since we needed special advertising to get this initial season off to a good start, we've hired her to be the manager and public relations officer for the tree farm. Julie majored in Business Management at college but this will be her first job. We discussed the ad campaign over dinner and she has lots of interesting ideas."

"Did Julie have this same epiphany as you? If not, you might want to take some time to think this through."

"I not sure about that but I do know she didn't act repulsed by my manly charms. Seriously, I'm not assuming anything about a woman. Your minds don't work like ours. I plan on getting to know the lady over the next month or two and then I'll know if the feelings are mutual. But right this minute if Julie wanted the moon and the stars, I'd find a way to deliver them."

"That sounds very romantic. I've got to get some sleep so I'll talk to you later. Keep me posted on this Julie saga. Goodbye, Scott." Diana hung up the phone and smiled to herself. She knew that she didn't have to wonder any longer if Scott would ever find contentment in his personal life. Scott had just discovered a profound truth. Love was all about giving instead of taking.

CHAPTER FIVE

Julie awoke before sunrise the next morning trying to remember her dreams from the previous night. Since she couldn't sleep, she decided to get up and shower before making breakfast. Maybe a pot of strong coffee would help shake off the sluggishness she felt after such a restless night.

It had been past midnight before she had managed to climb into bed. But the minute she closed her eyes, she saw black hair that made her fingers itch to brush the curls away from those chocolate colored eyes. When she had finally managed to fall asleep, her dreams had taken up where her imagination had left off.

After a quick breakfast of toast and marmalade washed down by several cups of black coffee, she decided to call Aimee before she went shopping. She needed to get another female's perspective about these feelings she was having about a certain gentleman. *Aimee had dated more so maybe she could explain why I'm feeling confused and excited at the same time.*

The phone rang several times before a sleepy voice came on the line. "Hello."

"Aimee, it's Julie."

After squinting at the clock on the bedside table through only one eye, Aimee replied.

"Is the townhouse on fire? Is someone sick? Anything else can wait until later in the morning."

"I'm sorry, Aimee. I didn't even look at the time. There's no emergency. I've been up for hours and assumed you were awake, too. I'm just having a panic attack about my new boss. We decided that it would be best to set up an office at the country house and that means I'll be seeing Scott every day."

"That's right! The dinner party was last night, wasn't it? What was he like? Was he attractive?"

"A more accurate term would be magnificent. The man could have been the model for those Greek statues of yours. One touch of his hand and I was ready to melt into his arms."

"There was touching? You, go girl!"

"Just a handshake but that was enough to make me realize the danger he poses to my will-power. Any suggestions on how to control my crazy impulses to give him whatever he wants?"

"My advice is to enjoy the moment. You may never have another chance and he could be the perfect man for you."

Together with John and Mary, Julie spent several hours in the office supply store buying the items needed to turn the guest room into an office. Julie was checking items off a list she had made before leaving the townhouse earlier that morning. Wooden desk with several file drawers, printing calculator, stapler, tape dispenser, computer, monitor, printer, scanner/fax/copier combo, multi-line business phone with messaging capabilities. Next, came the supplies needed to operate all of them.

As John surveyed the shopping carts piled high with their purchases, he decided that a small moving van would be needed to transport the desk and everything else to the farm.

"While you're getting your personal things reloaded in the SUV, I'll rent a van and pick up the desk and all the equipment from the store. That way if we need to put some of the excess furniture in storage, we'll already have the van instead of having to make a second trip. That shouldn't take more than an hour. Can you girls be ready to leave for the farm by then?"

"Sure. We'll pick something up at the deli for lunch. We can eat as soon as you get home and be on our way to Connecticut by early afternoon," Mary assured him.

"That should give me plenty of time to reload the SUV. After lunch, I want to pick up some extra supplies for the pantry and some cookbooks. I plan to experiment with some new recipes in my spare time. I'll meet you at the farm."

The drive into the country was a pleasant one. The trees were still sporting their wonderful fall colors. Red, orange, and yellow leaves adorned the trees along the road. Fall was Julie's favorite time of year. Warm days and brisk nights. Nights made for relaxing in front of a fireplace with soft music and a good mystery novel. Nights made for snuggling. *Where that thought had come from?* Julie wondered. *Probably from sleep deprivation since you couldn't stop thinking about Scott Williams all night. Go away!* Julie instructed her inner self. *You don't have time for romance. You have a business to promote.*

As she approached the tree farm driveway, Julie noticed the gateway sign. She had seen the sketches but she hadn't seen the finished mural. The two trees on either side of the driveway looked like bookends. An advertising plan sprang full-blown into her mind. A tree decorating party would be an excellent way of introducing the tree farm and its purpose to the community. Make the community feel like one big family. They could invite children and their parents from the neighboring towns, print up brochures to explain the donation plan and ask for suggestions on locations for the trees. Good will and good advertising. After she got the office organized, she'd get Scott's opinion on the idea.

Scott was sitting in one of the chairs on the porch of the Jones house waiting for Julie to arrive and wondering why he had agreed to relay John's message in person instead of leaving a note on the door. *Face the facts, man. Any opportunity to see Julie was too good to pass up.*

John had called to let him know that they would be delayed because of a flat tire on the moving van. But, he was a little confused. Why hadn't John simply called Julie on her cell phone he had insisted she get?

When she had gone off to college, John hadn't wanted her to get stranded somewhere without having a way of getting in touch with him. Julie was more like a daughter than a niece and John was very protective of her. It was a good thing that John wasn't aware of the kind of ideas he got whenever he looked at that same niece. His blood ran hot just thinking about her.

Scott heard a vehicle turn off the pavement onto the graveled driveway. That's probably her now. He watched as Julie drove up and parked next to the porch. She got out of her SUV, closed her eyes and took a deep breath. She exhaled it slowly.

Scott smiled at the little girl image she presented. What on earth was she doing? It looked like she was trying to commune with nature. It was as if the fresh country air was the first thing she wanted to put to memory. When she opened her eyes and grinned at him, he felt an emotional jolt that was like a sledgehammer hitting him in the chest.

"Hello. Where are Uncle John and Aunt Mary? They were bringing the office furniture in a moving van. I must have made better time than I thought if I arrived before them."

"John called and they should be here in about an hour. The moving van got a flat tire. He had to call a garage to get it fixed before they could leave the city. Do you want to unload your things while we wait?"

"Sure. I'll bring in the kitchen supplies if you'll start on the boxes in the cargo area. If you're not sure which room they should go in, just stack them in a corner of the living room. I'll unpack them tomorrow." Julie began taking out the bags of groceries.

They worked quickly. Julie was on her way back to the SUV for the last bag of groceries when she noticed Scott leaning into the vehicle to pull a box toward him. She stopped for a minute to admire the view.

As good as Scott had looked last night, he was even more distracting in a short-sleeved t-shirt that showed off all those muscles and a pair of faded jeans that showed off his sexy body. They didn't leave any doubt that he was a male. The butterfly sensations in her stomach had her hurrying to the other side of the SUV.

Soon all the boxes were unloaded and stacked in various rooms in the house. Scott stood watching Julie unpack a box of kitchen items. China and glassware were placed in the hutch that stood against one wall of the dining area. Then silverware, mixing bowls of all sizes, pots and pans were placed on the kitchen counter. Then came the cookbooks. Julie had either been collecting them for years or she had bought a copy of every volume the bookstore had in stock.

For someone who had obviously been pampered her whole life, she looked right at home as she arranged the cupboards. Soon the box was empty and Scott moved it to the back deck. He'd break it down for storing later.

"Would you like something to drink? I have bottled water, soft drinks or coffee," Julie asked Scott as returned from placing the box outside.

"I'll take a soft drink if you'll join me. You've been rushing around for the last thirty minutes getting the kitchen organized. If you don't take a break, you'll be exhausted before the van even gets here."

Julie handed Scott a can of soda and chose a blackberry-flavored water for herself. They went out to the front porch and sat down in the rocking chairs in contented silence.

Julie had forgotten how different the country was from the city. No blaring horns or tires screeching on pavement. The only sounds to be heard were the peaceful sounds of birds chirping and wind rustling the leaves in the trees next to the house. But as nice as the silence was, it only increased her awareness of the man sitting close to her. She was trying to think of something intelligent to say when Scott's cell phone rang. He excused himself, answered it, and went to stand at the end of the porch. That gave her an opportunity to observe him without being so obvious.

Scott was handsome in a rugged, masculine way. The physical work of unloading the boxes had made one lock of hair fall onto his forehead. She was filled with an intense desire to smooth it back into place. The slight cleft in his chin was begging to be kissed. The dark brown color of his eyes reminded her of her favorite chocolates. Dark and a little mysterious. You never knew what flavor of sweet cream was inside until you tasted it. She watched in fascination as a dimple appeared and disappeared in his cheek as he talked to the person on the phone.

It wasn't fair that the only man to turn her on in years was someone she should resist.

Julie shook her head to clear away the wanton thoughts she shouldn't be having and certainly couldn't act upon since her aunt and uncle would be here any minute.

Scott laughed as if something had either amused or pleased him about his phone conversation. *It must be a woman.* The rush of irritation that Julie experienced at that possibility almost felt like jealousy. Since she had just met the man, it was a totally ridiculous reaction. Julie rose from her chair and walked down the steps toward her SUV. She needed to make sure she had gotten everything out and to get control over these irrational mood swings. She had just closed the door when the moving van turned into the driveway.

John and Scott unloaded the equipment boxes and placed them on one end of the porch.

Next came the heavier items. Julie had chosen a wooden desk because she had wanted to make the room feel more like a study than a business office and the matching stand was designed to hold the computer, monitor and printer in the minimum amount of space.

"Do you know which area of the room you want this desk? That way we won't have to lift it more than once." John asked Julie.

"Yes, the desk needs to be in front of the back window with the computer stand on the right-hand side for easy access to the phone jack."

Julie and the two men worked for the next couple of hours arranging the furniture and office equipment while Mary put the groceries Julie had bought in the pantry and started their dinner. They had just finished hooking up the computer system when Mary came into the office. She marveled at the speed with which they had gotten the office organized. Except for a few boxes of office supplies, the office looked ready for business.

"I think you three should take a break." Mary set down a tray containing coffee and cookies.

"That's a good idea. We've gotten all the heavy items situated. The only thing left to do is get the files organized but I can do that later tonight," Julie replied quickly.

After everyone had filled their coffee cups and helped themselves to cookies, Julie looked around the guestroom-turned-office. It was just the right size for a one-man, or in her case, a one-woman staff.

38

The desk and computer stand occupied one corner of the room. Her aunt was sitting behind the desk testing the swivel action of the chair. Scott and her uncle were sitting in the wing chairs she'd placed in front of the desk for visitors. They'd moved the futon, which had been in the room originally, against the adjacent wall. It created a cozy atmosphere while providing additional seating and an extra sleeping area if needed. Some big, fluffy throw pillows for the futon and a few more paintings for the walls would complete the decorating scheme.

"Is that your famous beef stew I smell cooking?" Julie asked her aunt. Mary might have given Scott the impression that it was her mother's genes that were responsible for her cooking skills but it had been Aunt Mary who had showed her how to cut out all those cookies through the years.

"Yes, it is. I thought that would be something easy and it could cook unattended in the crock-pot while we give you a tour of the tree farm. The walk will help give you some ad ideas and getting out in the fresh air will improve everyone's appetite."

The four of them left the house and walked down the road that led to the tree farm. As they walked, Scott was explaining to Julie the care needed for the various stages of growth, from saplings to full-grown trees. In the first section were the trees that would be available to the public this season. They were identical in shape with only slight variations in height. With trees of such excellent quality, the public would have no problem picking out a nice tree for their holiday celebrations.

"Scott, why don't you show Julie the trees we've designated for donation? Mary and I want to inspect the new sapling area before we head back to the city."

"Okay. We'll meet you back at the house in an hour. The special trees are this way."

Scott led Julie up the access road.

John and Mary watched as Scott and Julie walked toward the back section of the farm. Scott was explaining something to Julie with an occasional question from her. He looked like a little boy showing off a new toy to his buddies. They were talking as easily as two old friends. They were so engrossed in conversation that they walked right past the donation section.

Scott quickly looked around to see if John and Mary had noticed his preoccupation with Julie. They were standing together and it looked suspiciously like they were plotting something.

He raised his hand and waved at them like he was saying goodbye. He only hoped that they'd think that was why he had stopped so abruptly. John waved back and turned to speak to Mary.

"I think your plan to throw those two together is working well." John chuckled softly.

Like it was yesterday, John could remember what it was like when you first met that special person that you wanted to impress. To be completely oblivious to the sights and sounds around you because you were only aware of the woman who was walking by your side. The one woman you didn't want to forget. Especially when you'd just realized she was the light of your life. The reason he could relate to Scott's distraction was because the woman who had captured his heart all those years ago was still walking beside him. With a loving look, he took Mary's hand and started down the road that led to the sapling section.

CHAPTER SIX

Julie was sitting in the newly created office of The Good Samaritan Tree Farm trying to put her advertising thoughts down on paper. There were so many little things to get organized and finished by the grand opening weekend that she'd need to make a priority list in the morning. Number one on the list would be checking the Internet for websites to order tree decorations. That should keep her busy all morning, maybe even all day, which was exactly what she needed. She intended to keep herself so occupied with advertising details that she wouldn't have time to think about her new colleague and neighbor. Scott Williams was entirely too sexy for her peace of mind.

Everyone had left an hour earlier and the silence of the house was a little unnerving. The ticking of the mantle clock sounded as loud as the beating of a tom-tom. Julie's imagination was magnifying every little sound way out of proportion. This was the first time she had lived completely alone and she wasn't sure she found her own company all that appealing.

It was also her first professional position. Even thought the business was co-owned by her aunt and uncle, Julie wanted to do the very best job possible to prove that she was capable of contributing to the success of a new business. To be part of a team that was trying to make a difference in the lives of two very important groups of people, the children of today who would be running this country tomorrow and the elderly who had given so much yesterday to make the world of today possible. They needed to know that their sacrifices hadn't been forgotten by everyone.

Julie wanted to prove that she hadn't gotten the job simply because she was related to the boss, for Uncle John's sake as well as her own. If she managed to impress her hunky new boss with her business acumen in the process, she would consider it an added perk. Although, Scott did say her cheesecake would be all it would take to keep him happy.

It would seem that her mind had a stubborn streak because it kept coming back to the subject of Scott Williams. *You're a hopeless case. This fascination with Scott is bordering on obsessive,* Julie told herself sternly.

While they were looking at the trees this afternoon, she had explained her promotional ideas to Scott. He had agreed that a decorating party was a good plan and the use of suggestion boxes to get the names of needy families in the community would be very helpful. Her theory was really very simple. By giving the residents in the surrounding communities the opportunity to be a part of the donation process, they would be more apt to buy a tree for their own homes.

They could ask for volunteers to help decorate the trees after they were delivered. Who knows? Maybe, seeing all the children who needed a loving family would make some of the couples think about adoption. That would be the ultimate present for those boys and girls.

She had enjoyed talking to Scott. It had helped to clarify her ideas to discuss them with him and get his feedback. Julie knew they were going to make a good team. A good working relationship was essential to making a business run smoothly. Scott had offered suggestions that would actually make her plans work better. They'd been so absorbed in the advertising possibilities that they had walked right past the donation section. It had felt like they had known each other for years instead of days. It was amazing how they seemed to be on the same wave-length about things. It was almost as if they shared the same thoughts.

Wow! That could be a little scary! She sincerely hoped that Scott wasn't privy to all of her thoughts, because some of them were becoming x-rated. Especially the ones about him. Regardless of how many times she told herself that any relationship between them other than friendship was out of the question, her stubborn heart wanted to argue the point.

While the logical part of her brain told her friendship was the only practical relationship they should have, the emotional part couldn't keep thoughts of a much friendlier relationship out of her head. An intimate relationship that involved lots of caressing, running fingers through silken hair and kissing sensual lips. She wasn't sure if she had enough will power to resist all that tempting testosterone.

Aimee would get a big kick out of Julie's attempt to resist a relationship. In college, that had been the last thing on her mind. Aimee had set her up on blind dates. But there hadn't been many second invitations because the guys had gotten the mistaken impression that she wasn't very friendly. It wasn't that she wasn't sociable or didn't enjoy the opposite sex. The simple truth was that she hadn't been interested enough in the men to make an effort to charm them into sticking around. But with Scott it was totally different. She found him way too appealing.

She wondered if a good friendship could turn into something more romantic. She'd always heard that a friend couldn't be a lover. That it would change the rules completely and destroyed friendships. That just didn't make sense to her analytical mind. Wouldn't it be better if that special someone were also a person that you liked and respected not just someone who was physically attractive to you?

She wished that cupid, or whoever was in charge of love, would make his intentions clearer. It would be nice to know if a particular person who had just came into your life was fate. Your own special destiny. That way it wouldn't be confusing. *You can't solve the mysteries of life tonight, so concentrate on this ad campaign.*

She stared at the computer screen for a few minutes. It was no use. Her mind was a complete blank. Not one constructive idea. At least, not ideas about trees. She needed a break. Maybe a cup of Irish coffee would help.

As she went into the kitchen, the spic and span condition of the counter filled her mind with the image of Scott helping her with the dishes after dinner. She shook her head and smiled at the absurdity of finding such a mundane task romantic. It wasn't simply that he was such a handsome man. He was also kind, considerate and a good listener. All the best qualities you could want in a man.

Could he be that special one who was her destiny? Was she being stupid to pass up the chance of finding true love? She really needed to get some perspective on her feelings for Scott. The man's image was like a thick fog. It surrounded her mind when she least expected it to the point she couldn't think of anything else.

Julie finished preparing her coffee and went back to the office to turn off the computer since it was apparent that she wasn't going to get any work done tonight. She sipped her coffee as she began clearing her desk. When she picked up the ad file to put it back in the drawer, she noticed the notepad with the phone numbers that Scott had written down earlier before he had said goodnight.

Julie had walked with him to the door so she could lock up. Scott had turned to look at her with a concerned expression on his face. He had taken her hands in his and given them a soft squeeze. For a split second, she thought that he was going to kiss her but he smiled instead and spoke softly.

"Call me anytime, day or night, if you have questions or just need to talk to someone. It can get a little lonely out here if you're not used to the country."

"Thanks. I'll probably have so many questions that you'll regret making that offer." The disappointment she had felt when he hadn't kissed her was a little overwhelming.

She looked at the clock on the wall. It was after midnight. Was it too late to call Scott? Was he asleep already? These questions were running through her head as she debated whether she should call at this hour just to say goodnight. To have his voice be the last thing she heard before she went to bed. *Don't be silly. He'll think you've got a serious mind problem if you do something as foolish as that.*

When she found herself yawning, she knew the whiskey was beginning to relax her. It had been such a long day that she decided to go to bed. She was exhausted from all the physical labor of setting up the office on top of the restlessness last night. *You've got to get some sleep or you'll be a walking zombie tomorrow.*

Before she turned the lights off in the office, Julie couldn't resist the urge to take a peek at Scott's cabin. She pushed the curtain out of the way but she couldn't really see that much. The fir trees obscured the view. The only thing visible from her office window was the back deck and there weren't any lights on. It was comforting to know that he was nearby.

She hoped she'd be able to sleep instead of dreaming about Scott. As she got ready for bed, she told herself it was only a matter of closing her eyes and emptying her mind. Unfortunately, that's when her subconscious took over. As hard as she tried, she couldn't keep her thoughts from turning to her new neighbor. She remembered the way he had listened when she had talked about her ideas and the look in his eyes as he had stood at her door before leaving.

Scott had held her hand an extra minute or two when he'd thanked her for a pleasant evening and wished her a good night. That long silent look had confused her even more because it had simmered with the same longings that she suspected were in her own eyes. An intense longing for him to him take her in his arms and kiss her passionately.

It might have been her imagination but Julie could almost see him struggling between what would be socially acceptable behavior and what he really wanted to do. It was that same look that was keeping her awake because it had made her realize that he was as attracted to her as she was to him. The knowledge that he wanted her made ignoring the growing attraction she felt for him even harder.

Why not just enjoy the attraction and see where it leads? a little imp in her head inquired. *You're both adults.*

Scott couldn't seem to get to sleep. Usually the workday tired him enough to make sleep as easy as closing his eyes. He'd tried changing positions and plumping up the pillows. Nothing was helping. He must have drunk too much coffee after dinner. His body was totally wired and his mind wouldn't slow down. There were so many thoughts running through his brain. Questions about what was most important in life. Questions that he couldn't answer.

After thirty minutes of tossing and turning, he decided to read for a little while. Scott picked up the book that was lying on the nightstand. It was the latest mystery by his favorite author. He turned to the marked page and started to read. When he found himself reading the same paragraph for the third time, he gave up on that idea.

Maybe a glass of wine would help him relax. He got out of bed, went into the kitchen, poured a glass of merlot and started back to his bedroom. Glancing out the kitchen window, he noticed that Julie's bedroom light was still on. *Stop kidding yourself. She's the reason you can't sleep.*

Was he the only one having difficulty sleeping? Was she thinking about him or was she still busy unpacking her things? He had carried several boxes of clothes into the bedroom but the one that he could imagine her opening was the one marked, 'Lingerie'. Little scraps of satin or a sheer white chiffon peignoir like the ones in the shop window in New York. Maybe, even a lace teddy. *Oh, man. He had to stop those kinds of thoughts. Think of flannel granny gowns buttoned all the way up to the neck!*

Scott had always been able to focus on the most immediate goal but he felt like his life was a mass of confusion. All the plans he had made for his future were scrambled up in his head. *Meeting Julie has turned your world upside down. Not in a bad way but certainly unexpected.*

For the past seven years, he had put all his time and effort into working on the farm and getting the trees ready for market with the sole objective of making the business a financial success. He had always assumed that he'd need to accomplish that goal before he could start looking for a wife and starting a family. Then he had met Julie. It would seem that fate had decided to throw a monkey wrench into his timetable.

He had really enjoyed talking with her today because Julie's business savvy had been a complete surprise. He'd never really thought of himself as a chauvinist but in his mind he had automatically assumed that someone as beautiful as Julie wouldn't take the time to develop her mind when all she had to do was smile at a man to get whatever she wanted.

Julie was a lot more than the country club debutante he had imagined. Yes, she was accustomed to having whatever money could buy but she wasn't pretentious. The questions she asked indicated that she had researched the tree industry while her advertising ideas proved she had a practical mind for business.

He had been so wrapped up in their conversation that he hadn't noticed that they'd walked right past the section of donation

46

trees. He had tried to cover this lapse of concentration by pointing out the need to keep the customers out of this section of the farm.

"We need to think of a way to prevent the customers from entering this area while making it something fun that will stick in the minds of the children."

"Why don't we have some wooden signs made with a picture of Santa's elves holding a placard that says "RESERVED FOR SANTA CLAUS," Julie had suggested. "We could cordon this area off with red velvet sections like an art gallery exhibition and put tin soldiers around to look like guards. When the children see the trees missing, they'll think that Santa Claus picked them up on his way to deliver the toys. We can include that service in the promotional flyers for the gift trees and arrange to deliver and decorate them after the children are in bed. It will give the children a little more Christmas magic to believe in."

"That's an amazing idea! Simple but effective. The children will be intrigued by the notion that Santa Claus delivers the trees and parents will treasure the joy and amazement on their faces Christmas morning." He tilted his head to the side as he looked at the woman beside him.

"What's going through you mind?" Julie asked.

"I was just wondering if you learned this problem solving ability in college or is it a natural talent."

"I'm not really sure that it's anything special. I did take a Creative Thinking course but I'm inspired by all this natural beauty around me." With a sweeping motion of her hand, Julie indicated the trees and clear blue sky. She turned to smile at him and noticed the way he was looking at her. A look that was filled with admiration and something else that made her much too aware of him as a man.

"Yes, I agree. The view is both beautiful and inspiring."

The country scene was nice but the beauty he was referring to was the woman standing in front of him. Every time they talked, he found something else to admire in this young woman who had never really known difficult times but seemed to have a clear view of the hardship of less fortunate people in the world. Julie really seemed to love children and wanted them to have fun during the holidays. She would make some lucky man an excellent wife and a wonderful mother.

I wonder what Julie's views are on marriage? Scott mused. *Slow down! You just met the woman. You're getting way ahead of yourself. She may not feel the same attraction.*

Scott had always prided himself on his patience but he was having a hard time ignoring his instincts. Those instincts were urging him to grab the woman, sling her over his shoulder and take her to bed where he could indulge in the fantasies that kept racing through his mind. For a few minutes he allowed himself to imagine what it would be like to slowly undress Julie one piece of clothing at a time, kissing the body parts that were uncovered until they both were in a frenzy of desire. Of letting nature takes its course.

He took a deep breath to slow down his natural reaction to those pleasant thoughts. As nice as they were, he knew if he didn't stop he would be up all night, so to speak. Logically, he knew that only time would solve his dilemma. He'd have to wait and see if Julie gave him any hint that she'd welcome his advances. He only hoped that he'd have enough self-control to stand the waiting. After a few minutes, he saw the light in Julie's bedroom go out. Before he turned to go back to the bedroom, he whispered, "Sweet dreams, Julie."

Scott was so preoccupied with thoughts of Julie that he failed to notice the twin pinpoints of light that appeared along the access road that ran past the donation section. The lights were very small but in the darkness they shone as brightly as the northern star.

Silently, two figures were walking toward the fence that edged the property. They were pushing a wheelbarrow that contained something large and bulky. When they approached the fence, the larger figure pulled a pair of pliers out of the back pocket of his worn jeans and used them to untwist the wire next to the corner post. It only took a few minutes for the wire to fall down to the ground. The second figure pushed the wheelbarrow through to the outside and waited patiently while the wire was reconnected to conceal the opening.

"Do you think that they'll notice anything?" the little girl asked her brother.

"I don't think so, but we'll have to be more careful from now on because someone has moved into the house. If the lady looks out the back windows, she can see this corner of the fence. We don't want to get caught when we are so close to having everything that we need."

They walked a few yards across the field and stopped at the edge of the gravel road to make sure nobody was coming down the road before they pushed the wheelbarrow toward an old abandoned shack. It was so dilapidated that it looked like a good, strong wind would blow it over. After putting the wheelbarrow inside, they retrieved two bicycles propped up near the door and rode away into the night toward their house on the outskirts of Spencer City.

When they reached their house, they silently raised the window and climbed into the small bedroom that they shared. The boy put his finger to his lips to caution his sister. They listened for a moment to be sure that they hadn't awakened their mother. Then being as quiet as mice, they put on their pajamas and crawled beneath the bedcovers.

The boy knew his mom would be so mad if she knew they were sneaking out in the middle of the night when they were supposed to be asleep. But most of all she would be frightened. She was very cautious about letting them explore for fear that someone would kidnap them. He couldn't understand why anyone would want to do that but his mother was very serious about protecting them.

She was constantly reminding him not talk to strangers and to never let his little sister go anywhere alone. She had made them memorize her cell phone number in case of emergencies while they were at school with instructions to call if they noticed anyone hanging around that they didn't know. That's why they had to do their scavenger hunting without her knowledge.

He really missed his home and his old friends from New York City. He had gotten to practice baseball every afternoon and games on the weekends during the spring and summer. In this small town, there weren't enough boys in his class at school to have a team and even if there had been his mom wouldn't let him participate in after school activities or class trips.

He wasn't exactly sure why they had to move here but he knew it had something to do with his father. At least there weren't loud voices arguing or doors slamming here and his mother was beginning to smile and laugh again. That's why his sister and he wanted to make this Christmas special for her.

CHAPTER SEVEN

Scott awoke the next morning with a strange sense of excitement. It almost felt like the future had taken on a special purpose all it's own. It was the same feeling he had gotten as a child when a planned treat or outing was coming. Like a trip to the zoo with his classmates or camping out in the backyard with his friends. It only took a few minutes to remember why he felt this way. Julie Jones.

All night Scott had dreamed of what life would be like with Julie as his wife. To come home at the end of the day to discuss with her the work he hoped to accomplish and planning their future together. It was hard to believe that a person could consume all of his waking and sleeping thoughts after only two meetings.

As he rushed through his shower, Scott realized that the best part of the day was yet to come. He quickly dressed and went into the kitchen for breakfast. He found himself humming along with the radio as he fixed toast and coffee. The reason he was in such a good mood was because he knew he only had to walk through the tree farm to talk to Julie about business or just enjoy watching her face light up as she talked about the upcoming events she had planned. She had a unique way of making the most ordinary idea sound like the perfect plan for getting the tree farm established.

He knew it wasn't logical but he realized that being with Julie was the only place he wanted to be. Even in this new awareness of his feelings, he knew that he needed to take things slow. Julie was friendly toward him but he wasn't sure if she would ever feel the same way about him. He could tell by the occasional look that she wasn't totally unaffected by him but he would have to be certain of her feelings before he confided his dreams to her. Dreams that included a future together.

The first thing Julie heard the next morning was the sound of birds singing in the tree outside her bedroom window. They sounded as happy and excited as she did. Today was the first day of her life as a working adult. She pushed back the comforter and went to look out the window.

Early morning was a special time of day with the sun just beginning to appear above the trees and bathing the surrounding area in gorgeous shades of orange and gold. It was amazing how refreshed she felt. The country air must have a soothing quality to it. Even with all the work ahead of her, she felt oddly exhilarated. After a few minutes of admiring the view, she went into the kitchen to put on a pot of coffee to brew while she took a shower.

As she rubbed shampoo into her hair, she found herself humming a tune that had been running through her head ever since she had awoken. Where had she heard that tune? It was familiar because she knew all the notes but couldn't quiet remember the words or the title. It really irritated her when she had information on the edge of her memory and couldn't recall it. She knew if she stopped trying so hard to remember, the name of the song would come to her later. She finished her shower and walked back into the bedroom.

Julie opened the closet door and looked at the clothes hanging there trying to decide what to wear. Just exactly what did an up and coming businesswoman wear? She didn't know if she should dress casual for comfort or as an executive would. Casual won out. She took a pair of comfortable jeans and an old college sweatshirt out of the closet and dressed quickly. She could always change into something more professional if necessary.

She went into the kitchen, poured herself a cup of coffee and walked out to sit in one of the rockers on the front porch. She loved to sit in the early morning quiet before the rest of the world was up. It gave her time to contemplate the blessings in her life and give thanks for them.

It was such a peaceful place that she wished she could live out here in the country year round. Unfortunately, a larger city would have more opportunities to offer in the business world she had prepared to enter. *I'll think about the future some other time,* she told herself. Today, I'm going to concentrate on the challenge of helping get the Good Samaritan Tree Farm off to a good start. Sixty percent of all new businesses failed in the first year. It was important to establish a pattern for successful future seasons.

When Julie felt her stomach roil, she realized that she was getting hungry. She went into the kitchen and stood debating what to eat. There was cold cereal with fruit but that sounded so boring. She opened the refrigerator and looked around to see what else was available. Nothing was jumping out at her. Finally, she decided to bake some blueberry muffins.

She'd have a special breakfast to celebrate her first official day on the job. Breakfast on the patio would be the perfect way to begin the day. The weather would turn cold soon and eating outdoors would no longer be an option. She knew that she'd need to plan a more structured morning routine soon but she wanted to make this first day memorable.

While the muffins were baking, she rummaged through the linen closet until she found a colorful tablecloth for the patio table. The potted plant she had bought yesterday would make it more festive.

I wonder if Scott's had breakfast. Okay, Jones! It's time to get your attention on the job at hand. No more lollygagging!

Wait a minute. That's it! "Along Came Jones" was the name of the song she'd been trying to remember. It was the same song that Aimee would always sing to lighten me up and get me to relax. The song told the story of a Royal Canadian Mounted policeman who always came to the rescue of a damsel in distress. As she recalled, they always got their man. That was an interesting thought.

She was taking the muffins out of the oven when the phone rang. She glanced at the caller ID display before picking up the receiver. "Hello, Scott."

It was an eerie feeling to be thinking about Scott one minute and then have him call on the phone the next minute. It must be mental telepathy. *Wishful thinking,* a voice inside her head told her. If that's all it took to make the things that she wanted to happen, the really important things, she'd begin star gazing every night until she saw the next shooting star.

"Good morning. I wanted to tell you that I'm going into Spencer City this afternoon to pick up a machine part. If you can get the business flyers ready by then, we can distribute them to the local businesses. I'll introduce you to the merchants and show you the best places to post them."

"That's a good idea. Have you had breakfast yet? I made fresh blueberry muffins. I was just getting ready to eat if you would like to join me. We can discuss the flyer while we eat."

"Blueberry muffins with lots of butter sounds like the perfect way to start the day. I'll be right there." He realized that the fact that he could look across the table and see her smiling face while he enjoyed those muffins was the real reason he agreed so quickly to her invitation. He wasn't concerned with the fact that this would be his second breakfast today. He could work off the extra calories this afternoon.

When Scott arrived, he found the front door open and the mouth-watering aroma of blueberries wafting through the screen of the storm door. He knocked loudly on the doorframe and called out, "Julie? It's Scott."

"Come on in. I'm in the kitchen." Julie answered.

Scott walked to the kitchen doorway and stopped as if there was an invisible barrier that prevented him from entering. The domestic scene before him made draw in a deep breath to slow down the sudden increase to his heart rate. For one millisecond, that organ had stopped from the unbelievable beauty of this woman. Then it had starting racing so fast he was certain it would jump out of his chest.

Julie was arranging a basket with the breakfast foods. It contained muffins, a butter dish, dessert plates and silverware on a serving tray. On the counter sat another tray with a coffee carafe, cups, and a pitcher of juice.

"Would you mind carrying the beverage tray to the patio table? I'll bring the food."

"Lead the way." Scott told Julie. "Anywhere." He added softly to himself as he followed her out onto the cobbled patio and placed the tray on the serving cart by the door.

He looked around at the changes Julie had made to the small area. She had placed a bright blue tablecloth on the table. The centerpiece was a container of yellow and white pansies. It was amazing how a few simple things could change an ordinary patio into a cozy dining spot. If this was what it felt like to come home to a wife, he realized that the sooner he could convince Julie to marry him the better he'd like it.

Julie moved the flowers to one side and quickly transferred the items from the trays to the table. After filling the juice glasses and coffee cups, she turned to Scott.

"You're my first official guest, Mr. Williams. Breakfast is served." Julie motioned to the seat across the table as she smiled shyly at the handsome young man who stood staring at her like she was an oasis in the desert and he was in urgent need of water.

Scott bowed slightly and pulled out her chair. After Julie was seated, he moved around to his chair, sat down and picked up his juice glass. "To new friends and new beginnings."

After helping themselves to muffins, they ate in silence, each contemplating the peace of the countryside and their breakfast companion. It was almost like they had done this hundreds of times before in a previous lifetime. Julie poured them each a second cup of coffee and pulled out a rough draft of the flyer she had worked on last night. They talked about the various points that they wanted to get across to the public. With one or two revisions the flyer would be ready to be printed up into brochure form.

"Breakfast was delicious. Thank you for inviting me." He smiled at Julie as he pushed back his chair and stood up. It was their first breakfast together and he planned on doing everything he could to make it an everyday occurrence.

"Your welcome. I enjoyed having the company. I've never liked eating alone."

"Me either. I've recently discovered that most things are better if they're shared with someone." Scott realized that his heart was in his eyes as he looked at Julie but he didn't have the willpower to pretend at the moment.

"I hate to eat and run but I need to get some things done this morning. Will you have enough time to get the brochures printed up before we go into town this afternoon?"

"Yes, that will be plenty of time."

"Good. I'll pick you up at 1:00."

With a wave of his hand, Julie watched as Scott walked around the house toward the storage shed that contained the farm equipment. He must be in a good mood to be whistling a song about a snowman when there wasn't a flake in sight.

Scott couldn't keep a grin from appearing. Breakfast with Julie had been one of the most pleasant hours Scott had ever spent. It made him more determined than ever to make her his wife.

CHAPTER EIGHT

Spencer City was only five miles from the tree farm so the drive didn't take that long. The city limits sign listed the population at 1,275 but that census count must be at least ten years old. Main Street was only five blocks long and almost deserted. There were a few cars parked at the diner. A young man and woman were window-shopping at the jewelry store. Across the street from the Boone County courthouse, two young mothers were watching as their toddlers played in the sandbox section of the town square.

It was a peaceful, little rural town that was fast becoming a thing of the past. There just weren't enough jobs available to keep the young people from moving away. They were being forced to look for work in the larger cities. Maybe, the Good Samaritan Tree Farm would bring in some customers for the other businesses in town as well so they wouldn't have to close.

Scott gave Julie a quick tour of the town before driving to the equipment dealer to pick up the part for the trimmer machine. He introduced Julie to the owner, Jim Grant, and explained that she would be working with him at the tree farm this season.

"It's a pleasure to meet you, Mr. Grant. We're going to have a big party to introduce our tree farm to the community. We'd like to personally invite you and your family to come enjoy the festivities that evening. Scott and I wondered if you would mind if we left these grand opening promotion brochures for your customers."

Scott watched as Julie gave Jim one of those dazzling smiles of hers and almost laughed at the speed with which he cleared a spot next to the cash register. Jim Grant placed the brochures on the front counter and promised to mention the grand opening to all his customers.

Scott was beginning to think that just having such a charming young woman promoting the tree farm was going to insure the success of the grand opening. He paid for the part and waved goodbye as they walked to his truck.

"Are all the business owners as nice as Mr. Grant? If they are, we should have all these brochures distributed in no time."

"I don't remember Jim being quite that agreeable with me when I first moved here but then I don't come with the same equipment as you do. If you smile at all of the business owners like that, the ad campaign will be a complete success." Scott laughed when she blushed and protested.

"I was only keeping a positive attitude and being friendly. But as I recall, that approach worked on most of my professors when I needed extra time to complete an assignment." Julie's grin was full of mischief and the knowledge of her feminine appeal.

"Positive attitude, my foot. Those professors didn't stand a chance. Your smile could charm a man into doing whatever you wanted him to do despite all his good intentions."

"Does that analysis apply to you? Are your intentions good?" Julie raised her eyebrows in watchful waiting. She was certain that she had found a clever way to get Scott into admitting his true feelings.

Scott considered answering her questions honestly but decided to keep his intentions secret a little while longer. It wouldn't hurt to leave her wondering exactly what was on his mind. Instead, he opted for humor to diffuse the situation. He looked at her with a little smirk on his face that was calculated to infuriate any woman.

"I think I'll take the 5th on that subject. Right now we need to finish with this brochure campaign." He spoke with a solemn tone but couldn't keep a twinkle out of his eye.

They made several more stops at various businesses around town. At each business, the men flocked around Julie like strutting roosters and she was the only hen in the coop. Even the older men were acting like they had never seen a pretty woman that close before.

It was starting to get on Scott's nerves. His normally easy-going personality was being strained with the effort to not punch them in the face. Black a few eyes so they were so swollen that they couldn't ogle her. He pulled into the bank parking lot with a sigh of relief. He knew that the bank president wouldn't be acting so dumb. Jack Reed had to maintain a professional attitude toward the customers.

"I didn't think that banks allowed solicitations."

"They don't but we need to add your name to the signature card so you can write checks on the tree farm account. After we finish doing that, I'll treat you to dessert and a cup of coffee at Joe's Diner. The apple pies are delicious and Joe would never forgive me if I didn't bring you by to meet him." Scott told Julie as he opened the door of the bank.

They had almost reached the bank president's office when Jack walked out and saw who was approaching. Scott watched as a welcoming smile appeared on his face and he gathered Julie's into his arms for a big bear hug for a few seconds before turning to shake hands with him.

"Julie, this is a wonderful surprise. John told me you had moved into his country house but I haven't had time to call. I can't believe how much you look like your mother. It was like seeing Ellen waltz through those doors. I'm sorry. I didn't mean to get all sentimental on you."

"Don't apologize. It's nice to know that mom is still remembered by her friends."

"Scott, what can I do for you today?" Jack asked when he heard a throat clearing coming from the man standing by Julie.

"I need to add Julie's name to the signature card for the tree farm account. She'll be taking care of the public relations and grand opening event."

"No problem. Just go over to the accounts section and Jan will be happy to help you.

I'm on my way to a meeting so I can't stay and help you myself. It was so good see you Julie.

Give me a call if I can help you with anything else in the future." With a nod at Scott, he hurried out of the bank.

"I didn't know that you knew Mr. Reed so well." Scott couldn't keep a little bit of irritation out of his voice.

"He's an old friend of Uncle John, my father and my mother. The four of them grew up together. I think he had a crush on my mother when they were teenagers. I had forgotten that he had moved here from New York last year." Julie told him. "Let's get that card filled out. I'm ready for that pie you promised."

Since returning from Spencer City, Julie had been trying for the past hour to get the grand opening advertisement ready to put into the local paper and on the radio station but she wasn't being very successful. She couldn't seem to concentrate. Her mind kept wandering to this morning's trip. Julie had met some interesting people and it had been nice seeing Jack Reed again. He had been a frequent visitor to her uncle's house while she'd been growing up.

On the way into town, she had been a little nervous because she hadn't known what to expect from the people in such a small town. Maybe it was because she was with Scott, but the people had been friendly and welcomed her to their community. Their visit to the local diner had been the most fascinating. Joe Bosley, the owner, had been eager to promote the upcoming tree trimming party. He had placed the flyers directly on the tables so the customers could read them while they waited on their food. He had refused to let them pay for their food as his way of welcoming Julie to the community.

On the way home, Scott had taken the scenic route to show her a little more of the countryside and an alternate way to get to town. They had discussed types of literature, movies, sports, cars versus trucks and had discovered that they agreed on most subjects.

As Scott had pointed out landmarks, Julie had listening to the sound of his voice and let her mind wander back to their conversation in the equipment parking lot. She couldn't stop her heart from racing when she thought about the way his eyes had darkened to a deeper shade of brown as he had declined to answer her question about his intentions. It wasn't so much the good intentions he might have but the bad ones that excited her. *Get a grip, girl! You're acting like a teenager with her first crush. Get back to work.*

She was typing up the final draft when the office phone rang. She picked up the receiver and spoke in her best professional voice. "Good Samaritan Tree Farm. This is Julie Jones."

"Julie, can you come out to the access road? I want to show you something." Scott's voice sounded different somehow. Like he was distracted or worried.

"Sure. I'll be right there." Julie hoped Scott didn't notice how quickly she agreed. She was beginning to suspect that her eagerness to help was only a cover for her desire to be around him.

As she approached the access road, she saw Scott kneeling and examining the ground directly in front of him. Then he looked down the road to the east and then to the west with an odd expression on his face. He glanced up as he heard her step on the gravel surface of the road. The five o'clock shadow of his beard made him look so sexy that Julie had to clench her hands behind her back to keep from touching him.

"Come look at these tracks. Whatever made them appears to be going both ways on the road. I see one tire track and two sets of footprints on both sides of the road. The tire track is deeper on one side of the road than on the other side. The smaller set of footprints seems to be walking parallel with the tire track while the other set is almost directly on top of it. What do you think could have made them?"

Julie knelt down next to Scott to examine the tracks and footprints. She placed her hand inside the footprints. One set was only one hand length long and the other was slightly bigger.

"Because the footprints are so small, they must have been made by children. Have you had any kids helping you with the trees?"

"I haven't even had any visitors with kids. I noticed similar footprints a few days ago that I assumed were kids using the access road as a detour. Now, I'm beginning to get concerned because of the tire tracks."

"The track doesn't look exactly like a bicycle tire. It looks more like a utility cart or wheelbarrow. Do you use either of those in your maintenance of the trees?"

"No," Scott answered as he shook his head in denial. "The tractor cart has bigger tires." He stood up and they began walking

down the road in the same direction as one set of footprints. They led
to the fence on the west side of the property. Scott and Julie followed
the tracks to the corner directly behind her house. When they reached
the fence corner, he began examining the wire sections.

Julie leaned over and looked at the ground on the outside of
the fence. "Everything looks normal to me but the tracks are on both
sides of the fence. How could that happen? Did they lift the cart over
the fence?"

"Wait a minute. Look at this." Scott pointed to the wire next
to the fence post. "It looks like someone has cut the wires then
twisted them back together on the outside so it wouldn't be noticed on
this side of the fence."

She looked at the wire Scott was examining. "That doesn't
look good at all. Someone went to a lot of trouble to keep us from
being aware of anything suspicious going on. Could kids think of
something this elaborate or did they have adult help?"

"I don't know but I'm going to check out the rest of the tree
sections for signs of trespassing. I need you to return to your house
and keep an eye on this area from the office while I'm gone. I'll do
surveillance on this fence corner later tonight. Just before it gets dark,
I'll walk up the driveway and watch from the window in your office."

As he turned to walk away, Julie reached out and touched
Scott's arm to get his attention.

"If you find more footprints, don't do anything without calling
me, okay? The footprints look innocent enough but appearances can
be deceiving especially if those kids aren't in this alone. We may
need to call the local sheriff."

Scott didn't think there was any danger involved in the
footprints so the anxious look in Julie's eyes and the concerned tone
surprised him. But it was proved one thing. The lady did feel
something for him. Was it fear for an acquaintance or was it concern
for a man she loved?

"Don't worry. I'll be careful." Scott leaned down and kissed
her on the cheek before he walked down the road. He tried to
concentrate on the footprints he was following but he could still feel
the softness of Julie's cheek on his lips. That innocent contact had
caused a spear of desire to go straight to his groin.

Julie walked back to the house and tried to finish the newspaper ad but she was distracted by thoughts of Scott and his sleuthing. She kept wondering if he had found any more footprints. Who could be responsible and would they be dangerous if confronted?

She was also a little nervous about seeing him later. She couldn't help it. This attraction to Scott was growing by leaps and bounds. She could still feel the contrast between the softness of his lips and the scrap of his beard on her cheek.

Julie knew that she needed to strengthen her resolve and resist her nature inclination to encourage Scott. A relationship between them could have an adverse effect on the business as well as the friendship he had with her aunt and uncle. If Scott and she got involved romantically and it didn't last, for whatever reason, her aunt and uncle would be forced to take sides. That would put a strain on their partnership that could destroy it completely. She couldn't let that happen.

Since she wasn't getting anything accomplished in the office, she decided to bake some cookies. That would keep her mind and hands busy. She got her cookbook out, turned to the cookie section and began taking the ingredients out of the cupboard. She measured, stirred, and shaped the dough then placed the covered bowl in the refrigerator to chill. She looked at the clock and made a mental note of the time to check on the dough. She was still too agitated by her thoughts to sit still. *I'll take a hot bath. Maybe that will help me relax.*

* * * * *

The driver, sitting behind the steering wheel of the dark sedan parked in front of the truck stop, was sipping a cup of coffee and looking at a map of western Connecticut. The PI report indicated that the person he was looking for was living in the Spencer City area. His room at the Hearthside Motel, ten miles to the north, was in easy driving distance. His salesman cover kept people from perceiving him as a threat until it was too late.

He started the car, backed out and turned out into traffic. It was time to visit that sleepy little town and check out the local law enforcement. In a one-horse town like this one, they usually only had one or two officers.

CHAPTER NINE

Scott spent the rest of the afternoon checking for further signs of trespassing. He didn't find anything, which was a big relief. That meant he only had to keep an eye on that fenced corner section of the property. It simply didn't make any sense. No trees were missing.

His route had brought him back to the front section of the tree farm and his cabin. Before he returned to Julie's, he'd call Sheriff Greg Rogers to see if there had been any vandalism reported around the county. He opened the back door, walked to the kitchen phone and dialed the county courthouse.

A female voice answered, "Boone County Courthouse."

"Hello, Sue. This is Scott Williams. Is Sheriff Rogers in?"

"Yes, just one moment. I'll transfer your call."

A few seconds later Greg Roger's voice came on the line. "Scott, what can I do for you today?"

"Greg, I've got a weird feeling that I've had some trespassers out at the farm the last few days. I found some footprints that look like they were made by children's sneakers. Since we're not officially open, there shouldn't be any footprints except Julie Joneses' and yours truly. Have you had any reports of kids hanging around where they shouldn't be?"

"No. Other than a few vagrants it's been quiet in the county. But, I'll check on all the local children. Since there aren't that many families with young children, it shouldn't take too long. Is Julie any relation to John?"

"Yes, she's his niece. We hired her to be the office manager and public relations officer for the business. She moved into John's house yesterday."

"Did you notify the Chamber of Commerce about adding her name to the contact list for the tree farm? Jason Clark will want to include an announce about the arrival of a new member of the community in the local news section of the Spencer Star. A little free publicity for the tree farm can't hurt."

"I introduced her to several of the local merchants when we were in town today distributing advertisement flyers but I completely forgot about the business listing. I must be getting senile. Thanks for reminding me."

"Think nothing of it, gramps. Just don't forget the poker game tonight. The boys and I want a chance to win back some of the money we lost to you last week."

"I'll have to pass on the poker game, Greg. I've got other plans for tonight. Give Julie or me a call if you find out anything or see anybody lurking around out this way. My cell phone number is 465-2312 and Julie's is 867-2546."

"Sure, no problem. Is the niece pretty? Married or single?" the sheriff inquired casually.

A little too casual in Scott's opinion. It made him suspicious. He had known Greg for a long time and considered him a good friend but he didn't want him getting any ideas about Julie or her availability.

"Never mind what she looks like, Greg," he replied a little too quickly. "I'll call you if I see anything else suspicious."

As Scott hung up the phone, he heard Greg laughing quietly. Too late he realized that Greg had been yanking his chain to get a reaction and he'd fallen right into the trap. Greg would tease him relentlessly now about his new lady friend.

After eating a sandwich, Scott decided to shower and shave before he returned to Julie's. It was only common courtesy to freshen up after a workday before visiting a friend. He told himself that he wasn't trying to impress her. He didn't want to acknowledge, even to himself, how important her regard had become to him in such a short period of time.

Just knowing he would be alone with Julie was making his pulse race. He needed to remember that he was going to Julie's to watch for trespassers not make passes at the woman. His mind wasn't having a problem remembering but his body seemed to have a different opinion. *Just concentrate on the job and ignore your instincts,* Scott instructed the part of himself that wanted to claim Julie as his own.

He walked up the driveway to Julie's and knocked on the front door. He could hear the sounds of Christmas carol music coming from inside the house. Several minutes passed before the door was opened.

"Come in," Julie told him.

When he walked in the house, he inhaled deeply. It smelled like fresh baked cookies. The aroma was making his mouth water and his stomach rumble. He followed Julie as she walked back toward the office and sat down behind her desk.

"I've just finished drafting the ad for the newspapers and radio spots. I need to get the copy to them by Thursday to make sure it appears in next Sunday's edition and for the radio station to air them next week." Julie pressed the print button on the monitor screen, waited for the document to print, and handled it to Scott.

"Read this and tell me what you think of it. I want to catch the reader's attention and make them curious enough to come to the decorating party next weekend."

While she watched Scott read the ad copy, she noticed that his hair was a little damp and the ends were curling slightly over the cowl collar of his Shetland sweater. He had obviously taken time to shower and shave. The smell of his cologne was enticing. His clean-shaven face was very handsome but she'd liked the five o'clock shadow he had earlier that afternoon better. He had looked so sexy that she'd wanted to run her fingers through his hair and make love with him right there in the middle of the tree farm. Thoughts like that weren't going to help her keep their relationship on a strictly business basis.

Scott looked up from reading the ad to catch an odd expression in Julie's eyes. It was a look of female speculation that made him wonder if she was as interested in him as he was in her. He

67

could almost feel the battle being waged between his heart and his head.

That look in Julie's eyes sure looks like a green light. Go for it, his heart urged.

No. *You need to wait. Remember your vow to take it a slow until you're sure about Julie's feelings,* his mind reminded.

But what if Julie's waiting for the same sign from you? Do you really want to waste this golden opportunity? A little imp in his head argued.

You have to resist temptation. Remember those footprints are important. There'll be another day to win the lady's heart. His good angel answered.

After this internal debate, Scott ignored the question that was on the tip of his tongue and smiled at her instead.

Oh, I'm in big trouble, Julie told herself. That smile was making the butterfly sensations in her stomach intensify and sending shivers up her spine. She watched his mouth as he talked and fantasized about how it would feel if those lips were pressed against her skin.

"I like it. The prize drawings for special wish trees for some families in the community are a good idea. There are usually a few families who can barely afford to buy gifts let alone a tree to put them under. This way it can be an anonymous way to make a child's wishes come true for the holidays. You seem to have a knack for public relations."

"Thanks. I'll go make a fresh pot of coffee for you." She needed to get away from the cozy atmosphere of the office before she acted on the impulse to kiss those soft lips.

Scott watched as Julie walked out of the office toward the kitchen. He was getting a little uneasy about this surveillance idea. It would be nice to catch whoever was trespassing but being alone with Julie tonight probably wasn't the smartest thing. He really should watch the fence corner alone because Julie was a serious distraction. That kiss earlier today had been a mistake. Instead of making the sexual tension less it had only made him want to give her a real kiss, right here, right now. It was becoming more and more difficult to keep his hands to himself. Much more difficult than he had anticipated. Especially when she looked and sounded so excited as she talked about the ad campaign. He wanted to be the cause of that kind of excitement in her voice.

Julie came back to the office carrying a tray with a coffee carafe, a cup and a plate of homemade cookies. She placed the tray on the corner of her desk.

"I brought some cookies along with the coffee, in case you wanted something to nibble on later. I've been experimenting with a new recipe so I hope they don't taste too awfully bad."

"That's okay. I don't mind being a guinea pig." He had a twinkle in his eyes from thinking about some other places he'd like to nibble. Scott picked up a cookie and took a bite.

"These are really good. Are you practicing your cooking for any special reason? Like, a boyfriend? They do say that the way to a man's heart is through his stomach."

Scott nervously awaited Julie's response to the questions he had asked jokingly. It'd be a cruel twist of fate to fall in love with her only to find out that Julie was involved with someone. An honorably man didn't steal another man's woman.

"No, there isn't any special reason or boyfriend. I just like to cook. Of course, it will come in handy if I should get lucky enough to meet someone, fall in love and get married. I suppose that's every woman's perfect dream," she answered with a wistful look in her eyes. She shook her head to remove the image of a man's face. Scott's face.

"Would you like company or would you rather watch that fence alone?"

"Your company would be nice. Talking will keep me from falling asleep." *What happened to that plan to keep some distance between Julie and yourself?* He ignored that voice in his head and told himself that he only wanted to get to know her better.

"I'll go get another cup for myself and be right back."

Even after Julie had left the room, he could still feel her presence. The fragrance she wore reminded him of the smell of gardenia blossoms after a spring rain shower. When she walked into a room, it was like the sun breaking through the clouds on a wintry day.

Julie returned shortly and sat down on the daybed. Scott had moved the desk chair over by the window and placed the binoculars he had used in his forestry work on the windowsill. He appeared to be taking the trespassers very seriously.

"Now we wait and hope the trespassers chose tonight for their next trip." Scott told her.

"What will we do if they do return?"

"Follow them to see what they're doing on private property in the middle of the night."

CHAPTER TEN

While Scott and Julie were waiting on darkness to fall, Sheriff Greg Rogers decided to stop at Joe's Diner and get something to eat. It would also give him a chance to check out the last set of suspects. Joe Bosley had recently hired a new waitress who had a couple of kids. He'd seen them talking to her when he was in there last week.

He had checked on the other two families earlier. He'd discovered that the Smith kids were out of town visiting a relative and the Atkins boys were attending a private military school out of state. That only left the new kids.

When Greg opened the door, a bell chimed to announce that a customer had arrived. He walked over and sat down at a table toward the back of the dining area. On the table, next to the napkin holder was a flyer announcing the grand opening of the Good Samaritan Tree Farm. He picked up a menu and pretended to read it as he looked around the diner.

There were the usual regular customers having coffee and apple pie. The Adams sisters were discussing the latest mystery novel. A stranger sitting at the counter looking at a map of the state must be a salesman. There was a battered brief case and a wrinkled raincoat on the seat next to him.

The same little boy and girl that he had seen the last time he was in the diner, were eating cookies and drinking milk at a corner table while they did their homework. He figured that the boy was nine or ten and the girl was about seven years old.

Breanna Cone

The doors that connected the diner to the kitchen area swung open and the new waitress came out with a tray of clean coffee cups. He watched as she placed the tray next to the coffee urn and approached his table with a pitcher of water. After filling his glass, she took her order pad out of her apron pocket.

"Are you ready to order? Our special today is Joe's Chili with Onions and Cheese."

He glanced at her before responding to her question. The nametag on her pocket read "Amanda". She wasn't your typical waitress type. She was only about five feet five inches and looked too delicate to carry a tray loaded down with plates of food. Her uniform couldn't hide curves that were close to perfection. Honey blonde hair was pulled up in a ponytail that made her look more like a teenager rather than the mother of two children. Incredibly long lashes framed deep blue eyes. Eyes that were watching him with a wary look as she waited for him to place his order. That look made him wonder what the lady was really thinking.

"The chili sounds good. I'll have a draft beer to go with it." He waited for her to write everything down, then pointed to the flyer.

"The grand opening of the tree farm sounds like lots of fun for kids. Are you taking yours to the decorating party?" Greg asked. Out of the corner of his eye, he noticed that the children had stopped their activities and were listening intently to their conversation.

Since he was wearing his uniform and badge, Amanda knew that he was the local sheriff.

She had seen him in the diner before but she wasn't sure if she appreciated the interest he was showing toward her. Her ex-husband had left her with a distrust of tall, handsome men. The truth was that she didn't trust her ability to judge their true personalities.

"Joe hasn't posted the work schedule yet. I might have to work that night."

Amanda didn't want to give him any encouragement. But it would be good for the children to get out of their tiny house. They never complained about having to come to the diner every day after school. She couldn't afford to have a stranger babysitting them and they were too young to stay at home by themselves. Part of her wanted to give the kids this treat but the practical part knew that it would be too dangerous to be in a large crowd of people right now.

72

"If you're free, I'd like to take you and the kids to the festivities. It won't be a late night so you don't have to worry about keeping them up past their bedtime."

She looked over at the table where Sam and Sara were doing their homework. They had obviously heard the invitation because they had a look of eager anticipation on their faces. Maybe, if they were with a law officer, it would be safe enough for them to go and enjoy being part of the community celebration.

"Let me check with Joe about next week's schedule."

Greg watched as Amanda gave his food order to Charlie, the diner's cook, with a request to serve it for her when it was ready. She walked past the restrooms at the back of the diner and knocked on the office door. From inside the room, he heard a gruff voice answer, "Come in." She opened the door and closed it behind her as she entered the office.

"Hi, Joe. Do you have a minute?" Amanda asked the man sitting behind the desk looking at the computer screen. He must have been running his fingers through his gray hair in frustration because it was standing straight up in spikes. He looked like a crazed man at the end of his patience.

"Sure. Anything to take a break from this bookkeeping program. Computers are not my area of expertise. A ledger page and a pencil are more my style. What can I do for you?"

"I wanted to know if you've had time to do next week's work schedule? If I'm not on duty, the children and I have been invited to go to the grand opening of the tree farm on Saturday afternoon."

"Actually, I plan on closing the diner early that day so everyone, including the wife and myself, can go and enjoy an old fashioned Christmas tree trimming. If I can find a small one, I plan on getting a tree for the diner. I love the smell of an evergreen tree. Is your date with anyone I know?" Joe wasn't trying to be nosy. He only wanted to make sure that the man would be someone who would treat her with respect.

"Sheriff Greg Rogers."

"My, my, that's interesting." Joe commented with a smile that made his face look ten years younger.

73

It was a smile that made Amanda wonder what was going on in his mind. As she opened the door, she turned back to speak to her boss.

"After the dinner crowd leaves, I can give you some pointers on that bookkeeping program that will make it easier to navigate between the software screens. I majored in accounting in college. I was going to teach before I got married and had the children. But after I separated from my husband, I needed to find a job quickly to support the children and myself. This job was open."

"Thanks. I'd appreciate any help you can give me." He thoughtfully regarded the young mother. She was a good worker but he'd suspected for a long time that her talents were being wasted as a waitress.

Amanda left the office and walked back into the dining area. Sam and Sara had moved while she had been talking to Joe. While he ate his chili, they were now sitting at the table talking to the sheriff like he was an old friend. All six eyes looked up as she approached the table.

"Have you been bothering Sheriff Rogers?" Amanda asked her two young children.

"No, ma'am," they answered in unison.

"He's been telling us about when he was a little boy and how much fun it was to explore the forest. He built a tree house with a ladder and everything!" Sam told her excitedly.

She hear the wistful tone in her son's voice and wished that she could give him a normal little boy's life and the freedom to explore the town and the surrounding countryside. But it just wasn't possible.

"How would you like to go help decorate the tree at the Good Samaritan Tree Farm next Saturday? Sheriff Rogers has been kind enough to ask us to go with him."

"That would be so cool," Sam exclaimed. "Decorating a tree outside just like they do in New York City!"

"Can we bring a camera and take pictures?" Sara asked with an excited look on her face.

"The local paper will be taking pictures for the news section of the newspaper but I'm sure that the owners won't mind if you take some, as well," Greg told the little girl.

"Well, sheriff, it looks like you have three guests for the party."

The happy looks on her children's faces put a lump in Amanda's throat and she had to blink away a tear. She hadn't realized how hard it had been on them to stay cooped up in the house. When she remembered why she had moved to this little town in rural Connecticut, Amanda told herself that she really didn't have a choice in the matter.

"It's time to get back to your homework so tell the sheriff goodbye." Amanda told her son and daughter.

"Goodbye, Sheriff," Sam and Sara called out as they returned to their table.

"I'll check my schedule and call you when I know what time I'll be off duty that day. One more thing, Amanda, my dates usually call me Greg, not sheriff." He had a mischievous grin on his face that put a big dimple in his check as he pushed back his chair and walked to the coat rack by the door. That walk looked suspiciously like a typical male swagger.

Amanda loaded the empty dishes on the tray before turning and walking toward the kitchen. She paused to look back at the man standing at the door putting on his jacket and decided to shake up the overly confident sheriff.

"Greg, I'll be waiting eagerly on your call." She waved a hand in farewell before entering the kitchen.

Greg paused with one arm in one sleeve of his jacket and a stunned look on his face. Hearing Amanda say his name with a hint of flirtation in her voice made his stomach muscles tighten in reaction. He had to close his eyes and take a deep breath to get his thoughts back to business. He opened them and looked around to see if anyone had noticed his confusion. The only activity was the animated chatter of Sam and Sara.

Greg had never seen two kids more excited. It made him feel a little guilty because he had asked them to go to the party so that he could ask some questions and watch their reactions. The look of gratitude he'd seem on their mother's face didn't make him feel very good either. If he had to arrest them for trespassing or worse, she would never forgive him. He didn't know why that should bother him. After all, the county paid him to check out possible criminals and keep the taxpayers safe.

What did bother him was the fact that the lady acted like someone who wasn't telling the whole truth. Amanda had seemed very reluctant to go out with him. It was almost as if she were afraid. He knew he didn't have a reputation as a lady's man so she shouldn't have been worried about him making unwanted advances. It could be his nature inclination as a sheriff to be on the alert for suspicious behavior but Amanda was keeping something about herself a secret. I think I'll run a check through the FBI. See if anything pops up.

CHAPTER ELEVEN

Scott lifted the binoculars to his eyes and surveyed the fence corner and the surrounding area. Nothing was moving outside and it was so quiet inside the house that he could hear the ticking of the mantle clock in the living room. He could also feel his heart beating in his chest. It was thumping like he'd been running wind sprints. It might have been his imagination but he thought he could see his shirt billowing with each beat. It was torture, plain and simple, being in such a small space with Julie.

The table lamp beside the futon was casting a soft glow on her face that made fighting the desire to make love to her a physical ache. Knowing she was within arm's reach but off-limits was going to drive him insane. If he concentrated really hard, he might be able to keep these urges at a manageable level but he knew in his heart that his passion for this woman would last forever.

"Do you have any idea why someone would walk through the farm after dark? It's a little out of way to be a considered a short cut, especially at night." Julie whispered soft and low. She needed to do something to break the silence. It gave her too much time to think about feelings that were becoming harder and harder to ignore.

Her voice sounded so sexy, Scott had to grip the binoculars until the knuckles on his hands turned white. Before answering Julie's question, he lowered his hands and quickly placed the glasses in his lap to cover his body's sudden reaction.

77

"No, I don't have a clue. It has me puzzled because nothing seems to be missing. No tree or equipment. Sheriff Rogers hasn't seen any suspicious strangers in town so that only leaves local suspects. Because Spencer City is such a town, he knows everybody and there are only a few families with young children. That should make it easier to figure out which ones are the culprits."

He watched as Julie picked up a cookie from the plate and poured herself a cup of coffee. She paused with the coffee pot in mid-air and asked, "Would you like another cup, Scott?"

"Sure. This vigil could last for several hours. It's a safe bet that any trespassers will wait until they can be certain that the chance of being detected is less likely which could be much later in the night." He prayed that the caffeine would lesson his sexual agitation.

He extended his cup toward Julie. She placed her hand underneath the cup to steady it before she started pouring the hot liquid. When her fingers brushed the palm of his hand, Scott drew in a sharp breath. That simple touch had an instant affect on his already aroused body. Curls of desire low in his abdomen were shaking his resolve to keep his mind on the mysterious footprints. He didn't dare let his mind think about her hands running over the sensitive areas of his body. Scott counted to ten slowly while he willed his body to behave.

Julie filled his cup with coffee, placed the pot back on the tray and sat down on the daybed. She had heard that softly indrawn breath and couldn't help an answering sigh from her own lips. She sipped her coffee and tried to think of something that would take her mind off the tension she could feel building between them.

"How are your plans going for the decorating party? Have you gotten everything you need ordered? Do you need my help with anything?" Scott asked when he could control his voice enough to speak without giving his inner struggle away.

"I've ordered most of the decorations over the internet so it is just a matter of one of us being here next week to sign for deliveries and storing them in the equipment shed. Since you usually check the trees in the mornings, I'll schedule any last minute shopping trips I have for the afternoons. I'll need some tools, a screwdriver and pliers, when the elves and toy soldiers arrive.

And probably your help putting them together." Julie laughed because she knew how men hated to be ordered around. "I'm sorry, Scott. That sounded a lot like a managing female instead of a business associate."

Scott's eyes deepened to a darker chocolate and his smile was pure male as he did a slow and very thorough assessment of her figure. "Well, you're definitely a female. I noticed that the first time I met you. For the record, most men I know would jump at the chance to let you manage them."

He watched as Julie blushed slightly and the pulse in her throat beat faster. Suddenly, the temperature in the room seemed to have increased big time and his brain felt fuzzy as his blood took a quick trip south of his belt. He'd better change the subject before the situation got out of his control. His best intentions were quickly being out voted by his desire to hold her body in his arms and kiss her until they were both breathless. He took a deep breath to slow his pulse and tried to think of a safer subject of conversation.

"Have you heard from John or Mary today? When I talked to him yesterday, he told me they planned on getting here around lunch time on Saturday to help with the setting up preparations."

"Aunt Mary called earlier to let me know she would be making several different kinds of fudge and candied apples for the food buffet." Julie was grateful for the chance to turn the conversation back to a safer topic. That one sizzling look from Scott had almost caused her to abandon her decision to keep things on a platonic level.

"She's also bringing two large coffee urns and a heated, serving tray to keep the hot chocolate warm. Since you haven't gotten sick from eating my cookies, I plan on baking several dozen for the guests to enjoy while they decorate the trees. It won't seem like Christmas if there aren't dozens of cookies to munch on. Baking was a large part of our holiday tradition when I was growing up. Aunt Mary insisted that the cookies that were left for Santa Claus's snack be homemade ones."

"It sounds like you had a good childhood with John and Mary."

"Yes, I did. They were already my godparents so the change to guardianship was a simple legal matter after my parents died. Both set of grandparents were older and in poor health so they couldn't take on the responsibility of a rambunctious five year old. My mother was an only child so that made Uncle John my only blood relative."

"How did they die?" Scott's heart was full of compassion for the little girl who'd lost so much so early in life.

"I was staying with Uncle John and Aunt Mary while my parents flew out to Lake Tahoe for a second honeymoon. They were on their way home when their private plane developed engine trouble shortly after take off and crashed into the mountains. My last memory of them was laughter and words of love. They telephoned just before they left the resort that morning to tell me that they were on their way to the airport and were bringing me a furry surprise. I still have that stuffed bear in my closet. The Search and Rescue Rangers salvaged it from the wreckage because it had a card attached to it that read: 'My name is Fuzzy and I belong to a little girl named Julie'. I lugged it around for years. It's a little bedraggled now but I plan on giving it to my own daughter someday. But, that's enough about me. How about your parents? Do you have any brothers or sisters?"

"My parents are retired and live in Boston. I have older sister, Diana, who lives with her husband and two children in south Florida. Because of the tree farm work schedule, I don't get to see them very often. My parents take turns spending the holidays with either Diana or me. This year it's her turn. Mom and Dad will be here for the grand opening. They want a couple of trees, one for themselves and one to ship to Diana. They're leaving the week after the grand opening to drive down south."

His sister hadn't wasted any time confiding in their mother the news that Scott had met a woman that he was romantically interested in. He felt certain that his parents were coming to not only support his business but also to check out Julie. Regardless of how old children were, mothers never stopped wanting to protect them.

"I can't imagine spending Christmas where the temperature is in the seventies and you have to turn the air conditioner on in the car to stay cool and comfortable. For me the best part of the holiday season is sitting in front of a cozy fire with a mug of mulled cider or wassail while snow covers the ground like a white blanket."

"I agree with you. My favorite memories are of opening presents on Christmas morning, then going outside after breakfast to have snowball fights. Aunt Mary and I would gang up on Uncle John. I remember one year we got about two feet of snow and we made a snowman, complete with pipe and top hat," Julie reminisced with a sigh. "I missed that while I was away in college. I'm looking forward to enjoying that same kind of family fun with a husband and kids someday."

Scott could picture himself sharing those family snowball fights with Julie as he heard the longing in her voice for a family of her own. His imagination created the perfect life with Julie. He'd like to have at least one son to pass on the family name and a daughter who would be a perfect replica of her mother. The thought of creating those kids with Julie had his body surging to rock hard with amazing speed. If he didn't put some distance between them right now, he was going to have a permanent zipper imprint on a certain part of his anatomy.

He picked up the binoculars and slowly scanned the fence line again. He had been so mesmerized by Julie's voice that he had forgotten his purpose in being here this evening. The wind was causing the trees to sway but that was the only movement he could see from this view.

"I'm going out on the deck for a closer look. Try not to move around too much in case someone is watching the house for activity. I'll be right back." He was reasonably sure there weren't any visitors out there but it was a good excuse to get out of the office for a few minutes.

As she waited for Scott to return, Julie tried to analyze the feelings that his presence was creating. She was irresistibly drawn to this man. It felt like she had been reunited with an old and dear friend after a long absence. It'd been so easy to talk to him about her childhood. She rarely spoke about that period of her life to anyone. She leaned back on the pillows and closed her eyes and listened to the music coming from the stereo. Soft melodies always soothed her mind and helped her relax. Within minutes, she was sound asleep.

Scott opened the back door and closed it quietly. He stood in the shadows on the deck but he couldn't see anything from this direction either. It was almost midnight and any children were home asleep in their beds. He stayed outside several minutes until the cold air restored his body to a more acceptable condition.

Scott was convinced that nothing was going to happen tonight. He'd tell Julie that then it was time for him to go home while he still had the willpower to leave. He went back inside the kitchen and walked down the hallway toward the office door. What he saw there made him stop and stare in amazement.

Julie had fallen asleep waiting for him to come back. With her hair spread out around her head like a halo and her face in total repose, she looked like an angel. The emotion that slammed into his chest was so strong it was incredible. Any doubts about whether or not what he felt for her was love disappeared in that instance forever. The emotions that swelled in his heart were so overwhelming he could hardly believe it. He wanted nothing more than to marry her and protect her from any curves that life might throw her way.

Scott silently picked up the tray containing the coffee pot and cookies and carried it to the kitchen. On his way back, he stopped at the hall linen closet and chose a thick afghan. It was warm enough now but the temperature would drop before morning. He unfolded the afghan and placed it carefully over Julie's sleeping body and held his breath when Julie stirred. If she woke up and looked at him with those beautiful eyes drowsy with sleep, he wouldn't be able to leave tonight. When she only snuggled into the warmth of the woolen fabric, he released it slowly. That fact gave him an odd stab of emotion. He didn't know if it was relief or regret he felt that she didn't awaken.

Julie looked so peaceful laying there that Scott could have stood there all night watching her sleep. One silken curl was lying on her cheek. He carefully lifted it and was fascinated as it wound itself around his finger. Almost as if it wanted to caress him as much as he wanted to slide the rest of his fingers into that cascade of hair and tug until Julie was awake. He couldn't resist placing one soft kiss on her cheek. He quickly laid the curl on the pillow and left the room before his impulses overruled his brain.

After checking the lock on the backdoor, Scott made sure the front door would lock behind him before he shut the door quietly. He told himself that he was doing the right thing by acting the gentleman. He walked fast to keep his body from getting cold in the frigid air.

When he entered his cabin, he looked around. The house was exactly the same as it had when he'd left earlier that evening but it seemed emptier somehow as he walked toward his bedroom. He changed into the sweatpants that he slept in and lay down in bed but his mind was still churning from all the different things he had seen today. The footprints, the tire tracks and the fence wire that was so expertly reconnected.

The tree farm wasn't the only thing that concerned him. Anyone brave enough to trespass, could break in and try to steal something from the one of the houses as well. Was Julie safe in her house alone? If not, how was he going to convince her to let him move in with her without frightening her more than necessary? *Don't borrow trouble.* He closed his eyes and willed himself to fall asleep. The last thing he remembered was how beautiful Julie's face had looked.

CHAPTER TWELVE

The special fencing material Julie had ordered to cordon off the donation section had arrived Monday morning. Scott and Julie had carted everything out to the donation section by trailer that afternoon, including the aforementioned screwdriver and pliers.

It had been a lot of fun seeing Julie so animated as she helped him place the metal stands at the four corners and thread the heavy red cords through the holes to make a velvet barrier. Next, she had unpacked the elves, the tin soldiers, and their clothing. They had assembled all the arms and legs before attaching them to the bodies with only a few extra nuts and bolts. She had posed them so they looked both mischievous and on alert as they appeared to watch for Santa to land. After everything was in place, Julie covered all the figures with plastic sheeting to keep them as dry as possible.

The rest of the week had been so hectic that Scott's only contact with Julie had been over the phone to update her on the progress of his work and the little odd jobs she'd asked him to do for her. Shaping the trees and getting folding tables and chairs for the snack area had kept him busy. He had picked up several terra cotta chimneas to place next to the tables in the snack area. Julie's idea was to create a cozy atmosphere so that people could sit and talk comfortably while they snacked on the refreshments. More like a big family reunion than a public party.

The only time he had actually seen Julie was when she had driven by on her way into Spencer City for supplies. A wave of hands in greeting was as close as he had gotten to his own personal Achilles heel. He had deliberately stayed away from her to get some perspective on his feelings. The effort it took was driving him a little crazy. Even though he didn't want to face the possibility, he knew that he needed to think seriously about the real consequences of a failed relationship between them. If he made it through this first season with his sanity intact, then he was going to concentrate all his efforts to convincing Julie that his was a forever kind of love.

In the meantime, he could make sure that he treated her with loving attention everyday. Surprising her with special little things would let her know that she was on his mind and that he wanted to make her feel cherished. Then on Christmas Eve, he would state his case and hope his instincts about her feelings were correct.

Delivery trucks had been stopping daily with the dozens and dozens of boxes of tree decorations that Julie had ordered. There were so many of them that the storage shed was beginning to look like a party warehouse. He was putting a box of heavy-duty extension cords next to the light strings when he saw the sheriff's car drive up to Julie's house and park. Greg Rogers got out and knocked on the door. Greg watched him as he talked to Julie for several minutes. *What can he possibly be saying to her that would take so long?* Scott asked himself.

Julie was in the process of taking the last cookie sheet out of the oven when she heard the knock on the door. Since she assumed it was Scott, she answered the knock still carrying the cookie sheet and wearing her apron. To her surprise, instead of it being Scott, a large man with a sheriff's badge attached to the pocket of his khaki shirt filled the doorway.

"Hello, I'm Greg Rogers. Sheriff Rogers. You must be Julie Jones."

The wonderful scent of chocolate chip cookies was coming from the tray she held. The smell brought back wonderful memories of his mom and the afternoon snacks that were always waiting on him when he arrived home in the afternoons from school. The smell was so enticing that it was making his stomach rumble embarrassingly loud.

"Yes, I'm Julie. It's a real pleasure to meet you. Scott told me that you and he were good friends all through high school. He also mentioned that you were investigating the local children. Did you have any luck finding out who was responsible for the footprints?" Julie asked this giant of a man who had been Scott's friend for many years.

Greg had rarely seen any woman with such intriguing eyes. When she talked about Scott, they seemed to glow with a special vitality or the light of love. His old friend was a very lucky man.

"Nothing definite but I do need to get some more information from Scott. He wasn't at his cabin so I though maybe you would know where I could find him."

"I think he's at the storage shed putting away some boxes of decorations." Julie replied. "Would you mind taking his coffee thermos to him? He usually takes a break about this time."

"Sure, especially if you send an extra cup and some of those cookies to go with the coffee. I'm officially volunteering to be your taste tester. I wouldn't want anything to happen to my good friend. If you need any references, I can give you my mother's phone number. I'm sure she will verify that I've had lots and lots of experience and am eminently qualified." The wide grin that accompanied this statement made him look like a mischievous little boy and she laughed out loud.

"You've got yourself a job. I'm sure Scott will appreciate the sacrifice you're making on his behalf. Your payment for this service is an extra dozen to take home with you." Julie tried to keep her facial expression serious but she couldn't keep her lips from breaking into a smile.

Julie quickly returned with the thermos, two cups, and two containers of cookies. She handed everything to Greg and watched as he drove toward the storage shed. He seemed like a nice man.

Greg parked the patrol car and opened the door. He was gathering up the snack items Julie had sent when he heard Scott speak.

"Have you got any news on my trespassers or did you just come by to check out Julie?" Scott asked in a belligerent tone. The hostility in his voice surprised him. He had never acted jealous about a woman before. He had never cared enough before Julie.

"Good morning to you, too. I come bearing gifts my friend." Greg held up the thermos and the cookies. Scott's snarling comment didn't sound very friendly. He poured them each a cup of coffee and helped himself to a cookie before answering.

"I stopped by your cabin to give you an update on the investigation. When you weren't there, I assumed the most logical place to look for you would be at the Julie's house. A very pretty woman in an apron answered the door and told me you were out here. I can understand now why you've been too busy to play poker with us boys."

Judging from the glint in Scott's eyes, Greg wisely decided that teasing him wouldn't be wise or healthy today. Only a man in love would have such an intense reaction if he thought his territory was being invaded. He watched as Scott relaxed the fingers of both hands that had instinctively tightened into fists. A man's primitive urge to fight to keep a mate was still as strong as it ever was. From having joined his friend in a few skirmishes in high school, he knew that the Scott's opponent always got the worst end of the deal from those fists. Especially his right cross.

After seeing the lady in question, Greg could understand why his old friend had fallen in love so fast. She was a very attractive woman. As much as he loved to eat, the smell of cookies baking hadn't been the first thing he noticed when she opened the door. If she cooked as good as she looked, then Scott was a doubly blessed man. He took a bite of the cookie. It was still warm from the oven and literally melted in his mouth.

Greg was a little envious of his friend's good fortune because he was getting tired of his own company. When he got to his apartment each night there wasn't anyone there to welcome him home. No aroma of homemade cookies. Right now the silence of his apartment was only broken by the humming sound of the kitchen appliances motors and the only smell was his garbage when he forgot to take it out to the dumpster.

"I've checked on all the local kids. The Smith girls have been visiting their grandmother for the past two weeks and the Adkins boys have been at a military school since August. That only leaves two

88

local children who would fit the footprints you described. I've charmed the mother into letting me bring them to the tree decorating party." Greg punctuated the sentence with a cocky grin. He chose to ignore the derisive snort and derogatory hand gesture that Scott made in response to that remark.

"Are you sure she wasn't just taking pity on you? Maybe, she only wanted to keep on the good side of the local sheriff, especially, if she suspects her kids have been up to mischief."

"You could be right. That's one of the reasons I asked her and the kids out here. By bringing them back to the scene of the crime, so to speak. I'm hoping to get a reaction that will give them away.

The mother doesn't socialize much so they don't get to play with other children except at school. I've seen them at the diner waiting on their mother and they seem to be well-behaved children who wouldn't be out getting into mischief. Unfortunately, the juvenile courts are full of kids who don't look like troublemakers. The Michaels' kids probably just need something to do in their spare time to use up all that excess energy." Greg spoke impersonally but there was a concerned expression in his eyes.

"I might have an outlet for that excess energy. With the sales season almost here, I could use some part-time workers until Christmas Eve. That should keep them busy. They can start tomorrow and help us get the decorating supplies organized. I'll pay them $2.50 an hour."

"They'd probably love to help. Sam and Sara were excited just thinking about helping to decorate a tree outdoors. Knowing that they'll be helping will make them ecstatic. I'll talk to Amanda about them helping out around the farm after school. It will be a good way to learn more about them without appearing suspicious. There's something a little mysterious about Amanda and the kids. They moved here about six months ago but nobody seems to know much about them. Outside of work and school, I haven't talked to anyone who has seen them out anywhere. I don't think she's dating anyone in town."

"Is this professional nosiness or a personal interest you have in the lady and her past?"

Scott asked with the same teasing note in his voice that Greg had used toward him earlier.

"A little bit of both. She's easy on the eyes and one of the few single women around town my age," Greg replied with a sheepish smile. "I'll talk to you later."

As Greg drove back toward town, he decided to go by the diner and tell Amanda about the job offer. The diner was on the way so stopping by before he went to the office wouldn't take him out of his way. He tried to tell himself that his motive was to solve the mystery but he felt an overwhelming need to see Amanda and this would be the perfect excuse to talk to her. Besides, he needed to find out what time to pick them up tomorrow.

He parked his patrol car in the space allotted for him next to the curb. He radioed his location to his deputy before getting out. He walked up the steps and pushed open the door of the diner. Greg sat down at the counter and looked around. He didn't see Amanda anywhere. Through the kitchen door he could hear Joe talking to Charlie Smith, the diner's cook.

Charlie wasn't your usual short order cook. He was a retired prizefighter who had taken one too many blows to the head. After his last fight had left him with a severe concussion, the doctors had advised him to find another occupation before boxing killed him. Cooking was the only other thing he knew how to do. That experience had come as a ship's cook in the Navy many years ago but it was enough on the job training to land him this job with Joe.

Greg looked around the dining area as he waited for Joe to finish his conversation. There were only a few customers in the diner. The Adams sisters were enjoying coffee and apple pie.

Mary and Martha were retired teachers who had never married and lived together on the same street as Amanda. There was a copy of *Detective Digest* lying on the table between the sisters. They were arguing the points of one of the articles. Since their retirement, they had started the Mystery Lovers Literary Club. The only other customer was the salesman he had noticed last week. Today, he was making notes as he looked at his map.

When Joe came through the swing doors, he saw the local sheriff sitting at the counter waiting patiently. He slipped behind the counter before he spoke. "Hello, Greg. What can I get you?"

"I'll take a cup of black coffee. Is Amanda working today?" Greg asked with a casual look around.

"Yes. She went down the street to make a bank deposit for me." Joe filled a cup with coffee and placed it in front of the sheriff. He had noticed Greg talking to Amanda last week and wondered if the sheriff was seriously interested in the young mother.

"Amanda is helping me with the bookkeeping duties for the diner. In one week, she's mastered the software I've been trying to figure out for over a year. Maggie and I want to travel a little bit before we get too old to enjoy the countryside so I've decided to train Amanda to be my assistant manager. That way I'll know the diner is in good hands during my absence."

"That sounds like a good idea, Joe. You've been running this diner for as long as I can remember and deserve to take it easy for a change."

Greg had just picked up his coffee cup to take a sip when he heard the bell on the door chime. He looked around in time to see Amanda walking through the door. He just sat there staring at her with his cup suspended between the counter and his lips. He swallowed convulsively. His mouth was suddenly as dry as cotton.

Walking in the cold air had added a rosy tint to Amanda's cheeks. She had left her hair down and the wind had tousled the golden tresses into a tangled riot of curls. Since she was working in the office, Amanda had dispensed with the shapeless waitress uniform today and chosen a more professional outfit. The sweater and skirt she was wearing reaffirmed his opinion that she had a nice figure. Very nice!

"Hello. Isn't this a gorgeous day? I sure hope the weather cooperates for the party tomorrow evening." She smiled at Greg and Joe before continuing on her way to put the moneybag in the office safe.

It was the first time Greg had seen her smile so naturally and it had transformed her from a worried mother into a carefree and beautiful woman. He watched her walk down the hall and shook his head at the thoughts running rampant in his head. The effect her smile had on him was obvious to anyone who had eyes in their head. He cleared his throat and looked at Joe. He had the same look of wonder in his eyes. Greg felt a rising heat start in his neck and sweep upward as a faint blush appeared on his face.

"Her ex-husband must have been deaf, dumb and blind. I can't imagine any man being stupid enough to let someone that nice get away." Joe sent a sly look at Greg. "Amanda doesn't talk about it much but I get the impression that it wasn't an amicable divorce."

"Divorce has a way of making even the nicest people turn nasty and vindictive. The dissolution of dreams can be a big disappointment especially if there are children involved. That's one of the reasons I've stayed single for so long. I don't want to make a mistake and end up as one more unhappy court statistic."

"Maybe, you're just waiting for the right person to come along. That reminds me. I hear you're taking Amanda and her kids to the party at the tree farm tomorrow. She works so hard, without complaining, that it will be good to see her enjoying herself."

"Yes, that's the plan. Excuse me, Joe. I need to tell Amanda something." Greg slipped off the stool and walked toward the office.

Joe watched Greg hurry down the hallway and chuckled to himself. Oh, yeah, the man was definitely interested.

Amanda was seated at the computer entering the deposit into the bookkeeping file. She looked up as Greg appeared in the doorway. His khaki sheriff's uniform along with his dark auburn hair and hazel eyes made a nice addition to the décor of the office. She might not trust men in general, but Greg seemed to be one of the good guys.

And it didn't cost anything to look especially if they filled out their shirt like the handsome sheriff of Boone County did. Standing with one shoulder propped on the doorframe and his arms crossed over his chest made his bicep muscles strain the material of his shirtsleeves while the shiny badge on the pocket of his shirt emphasized those impressive pectoral muscles. A man in uniform had always appealed to the woman in her.

"Good afternoon, sheriff. Is there something wrong? Did the wind make a total mess of my hair?" She patted her hair because Greg was looking at her like he hadn't seen her before.

"No, no, nothing's wrong. You look…fine. I just came from talking to Scott Williams and he wanted me to deliver a message. He's looking for some part-time help with the holiday tree sales coming up. Scott wondered if Sam and Sara might want to work there after school. The job pays $2.50 an hour. I told him I would let you know about the job offer and you could call him later if they were interested. Here's a business card with Scott's cell phone number." Greg laid the card on the desk blotter and quickly moved back to the doorway out of harm's way. He had to resist the urge to touch Amanda's hair to see if it was as soft as it looked.

He couldn't stop staring at Amanda. How could a change of hairstyle and a little extra make-up create such a difference in a woman's appearance? The sky blue color of the cashmere sweater and woolen skirt made her eyes even more alluring. The cream-colored pearls around her neck matched the pumps she wore. The shapely legs encased in silk hose helped complete the transformation that reminded him of the rags to riches story about Cinderella. The funny thing was Joe Bosley didn't look like anyone's fairy godmother but Greg could definitely relate to being the prince.

Greg was suddenly glad that he was still single and considered himself a very lucky man to be escorting her to the tree trimming party. Showing up there with a woman who looked as good as Amanda did would make the other local men envious. Because he was usually on duty, he always went stag to these events. Some of the residents of Spencer City, mostly the men, assumed that it was because he couldn't get a date. He suspected a few of them even wondered if he was gay. He dragged his attention back to what Amanda was saying.

"Sam and Sara have been hinting about an increase in their allowance. They'll jump at the chance to make some extra money. I think it's important that they learn the value of working for money instead of expecting someone to give it to them." Amanda's replied vehemently with a glint of anger in her eyes. "I'm sorry. That's one of my pet peeves."

"I agree with you. Too many people today think the world owes them something. In my profession, I get to see them after they steal the things they want from other people."

I wonder what incident or memory caused such a fiery look. The woman had such a calm personality that such a passionate remark was out of character. Scott also wondered if the lady had other hidden passions. He could think of one or two he'd like to experience first hand.

"The after school job will be good for Sam and Sara. The only problem is how they will get there. I can't leave work to drive them and it's too far for them to ride their bicycles." Julie told him.

"I can help you out there. I usually drive out that way in the afternoons on my daily rounds and I'd be happy to drop them off at the farm. Scott wants them to start tomorrow afternoon and help with the party preparations."

"Are you sure it won't be an imposition to drop them off every day?" Amanda looked at Greg with a puzzled expression in her eyes while her mind posed all kinds of concerns.

Why would a complete stranger offer to drive her kids around? Did he suspect that she hadn't been completely honest with him? Had her ex-husband convinced him that she had taken Sam and Sara illegally? What if he was trying to separate her and the children for some reason?

"No. I go right by the tree farm on the way out of town to check for game poachers." At her reluctant nod of agreement, Greg searched for a topic of conversation that would allow him to linger. "It's supposed to turn cold later in the afternoon so they'll need to bring coats with them. You can't be too careful with the damp night air at this time of the year."

He was babbling like an idiot but he couldn't seem to stop himself. The change in her appearance had him behaving like a schoolboy. He was noticing all sorts of new things about her today. Things like how smooth her skin was, how soft and kissable her lips looked and how that sweater clung to the fullness of her breasts.

"I appreciate the weather information. I don't have time to listen to the news very often when I get home after work. Between the housework and helping the kids with their homework, my evenings are too busy to watch television."

Amanda pushed back the chair and walked toward the office door and stopped next to him. She was standing close enough for him to see the fine lines that were beginning to form around her eyes. Close enough for the scent of her cologne to be a serious distraction to his thought processes. Even wearing heels, the top of her head only came up to his shoulder.

"If you'd like, I can pick Sam and Sara up after lunch tomorrow and drive them out to the farm. That would give you a little time to yourself before I come back later to pick you up for our date." Greg had an ulterior motive in making the friendly offer. He could talk to the kids without their mother around and it would also give him time to be alone with her on their way to the party.

Amanda considered the sincerity she heard in his voice and decided that he was only being nice not conspiring with Bradley Michaels. She was being paranoid for nothing.

"I love them dearly but when they're around there isn't any quiet time just for myself. A whole afternoon alone sounds wonderful. I can indulge in a long, hot bubble bath without fear of interruption."

That remark caused Greg to get a vivid picture of bubbles sliding off her smooth skin and his imagination was making the stirrings of desire an obvious reality. He quickly turned and left the office before he did something stupid like offering to scrub her back. She would think he'd lost his mind or that he was one of those sex-starved, hormone-driven law enforcement officers who preyed on unsuspecting women. He wanted her trust, her respect, not her contempt.

Amanda watched as Greg walked toward the front door of the diner. She wondered what had made him leave so abruptly without even saying goodbye. He had gotten a really strange look on his face just before he'd hurried off.

Greg exited the diner so fast that he didn't see the speculation in Martha Adams' eyes.

Mary watched her sister's eyes gleam as some thought ran through her mind. She had seen that look too many times not to realize that Martha was concocting some plan that would be totally outrageous. She had been trying to keep her sister's mischievous behavior in line for years.

"Martha, you need to stop whatever chicanery you're planning right now. You're getting too old to meddle in other people's lives."

"It was just a passing thought. Nothing for you to worry about, sister dear." She didn't tell Mary that she was concerned about their young neighbor. Amanda and her children lived across the street from them and Martha considered it a downright shame that she didn't have some young man coming to court her. *Perhaps, I can hear a noise outside tonight that would bring the sheriff out to investigate. He'd need to talk to the neighbors to find out if they had seen any prowlers around.*

Greg stopped and leaned an arm in the window of the cruiser to pick up the cell phone he had left on the seat. He hit the speed dial #1 and waited for Sue to answer. When he heard her come on the line, he spoke before she could go into her practiced greeting.

"Sue, this is Greg. I'm leaving the diner but I'm going by my apartment for a few minutes. Call me on the cell if you need me."

He wanted a little extra time away from his eagle-eyed clerk. She knew him well enough to realize that something was bothering him. If she suspected he was attracted to a woman, she would badger him until he told her Amanda's name. Being embarrassed once around a woman today was more than enough for any man to have to endure. Amanda probably thought he was a regular dork because he couldn't think of anything better to chat about except the weather.

* * * * *

The man in the wrinkled raincoat was looking at the flyer announcing the Christmas tree decorating party surreptitiously. The flyer was face-up on the counter of Joe's Diner, but he didn't want to draw attention to the fact that he was reading it. He had overheard the woman agree to go to this community event. It sounded like the perfect opportunity to put into action a plan to fulfill his contract without putting himself in danger of being caught. In a noisy crowd of people, he could blend in easily. There would be any number of chances to stage an "accident" without it being obvious. He just needed to get a better disguise together.

"Check, please."

CHAPTER THIRTEEN

Saturday morning dawned with blue skies and the bright rays of sunlight were shining in through Scott's bedroom window. It looked like the perfect fall day but Scott sat up in bed and reached for the television remote. He changed the channel to check the weather. The forecast was for a cold front coming in later that night with only a small chance of precipitation. Julie had worked so hard on the decorating plans that he didn't want anything to spoil the event for her.

He leaned back against the headboard and closed his eyes. His thoughts returned to his visit to Julie's last night. She had looked so beautiful. It had taken all his self-control to leave. He had wanted to awaken her with a real kiss just like Prince Charming. But he'd been afraid that a kiss would have aroused more feelings than she was ready to share. That was why he had settled for just a peck on the cheek. *Time to get up. You don't have time to daydream.*

Julie had been a little disoriented this morning. Instead of being in her queen-size sleigh bed in the bedroom, she had awakened on the futon in the office. She had fallen asleep there while she had been waiting for Scott. She couldn't remember being covered with the afghan. Scott must have decided to let her sleep there instead of waking her up. Her hearted swelled with tenderness when she thought about him caring enough about her welfare to make sure she didn't get cold. The afghan had kept her nice and warm during the night. Either that or the dreams she couldn't seem to get out of her head.

In her dreams, Scott had joined her on the futon and shown her that the smoldering look in his eyes was only a prelude to the fire he could ignite between them. The dreams had been so real that she could still feel his hand as he caressed her check and lips when he had feathered kisses on every inch of her face before taking her in his arms and showing her how a man should make love to woman...tenderly and repeatedly. Scott had been a wonderful lover and had made her feel like a desirable woman. But only in her dreams.

Maybe it was time to take this attraction to the next level. *I wonder what would be the best approach.* She considered her options? A romantic, candlelit dinner in front of the fireplace or sexy lingerie? She had a little, black teddy that was guaranteed to get his attention.

She could plan a dinner and let things happen naturally or she could meet him at the door with a seductive smile that would let him know she was interested in more than friendship. With a heartfelt sigh, she pushed those fantasies to the background to concentrate on the day's agenda.

Scott was walking toward the storage shed thinking about all the things that would need to be moved out to the entrance area when his cell phone rang. "Hello, this is Scott Williams."

"Good morning. I'm elbow deep in cookie dough right now but if you need help later with the tables and chairs just give me a call."

"Actually, I've hired Sam and Sara Michaels to help today and a couple of hours after school each day until Christmas Eve. I figured they needed something to do and we can keep an eye on them. Greg is bringing them by after lunch. He seems to have taken a personal interest in the Michaels' family." Scott explained in a dumbfounded voice.

"Is that something unusual for a sheriff to do? I thought getting all the facts involved in a crime was the normal way to solve a problem."

"No, not really, but the fact that Greg's attracted to the mother is unusual. I've known him since high school and he spent all his free time hanging out with the guys instead of cruising for girls. He was the only football star in high school that ignored the cheerleaders to their amazement. It was amusing to see the lengths they went to try and catch his attention. Greg has always been shy around women. He couldn't seem to find his voice when girls were around."

"He didn't strike me as the bashful type yesterday when he came by looking for you. He wasn't here that long but he was pleasant and friendly. He had a sexy eyes and a nice smile. You know the oven must have overheated the house. I'm suddenly very warm." Julie told him with a soulful sigh. It was a little dramatic but she intended to give Scott the idea that there might be some competition in the neighborhood.

"Then you'd better open some windows or the doors to cool off." When he only sounded practical instead of jealous, she issued an invitation.

"I'm going to have a light lunch of soup and sandwiches ready at eleven-thirty. Uncle John and Aunt Mary should be here by then. You're welcome to join us."

"I'd like that. It will keep me from having to go back to the cabin. I'll see you then." He turned off the phone and put it in his shirt pocket.

Julie's comment about Greg's smile had him a little concerned. Taking things slow could be a big mistake. He'd have to keep an eye on the bashful sheriff. I can't have him stealing my girl right out from under my nose. *Maybe, you should tell the woman in question that you want her to "BE YOUR GIRL". Not just think it in your head,* the voice of wisdom whispered in his ear. The woman isn't a mind reader!

Greg was finishing up some paperwork when he heard the beeper sound of the email notice from his computer. He logged on and accessed the icon to reveal the screen. When Greg saw who had sent the unopened email, he wasn't sure if he wanted to read whatever the message might be.

He had put in a background check last week on Amanda Michaels to a buddy of his in the bureau. In spite of his interest in the lady, Greg needed to know if she had a criminal record. In his experience, people only had two reasons for being that anti-social. They were either hiding from the law or somebody.

He sat staring at the screen several minutes before clicking on the envelope to open the message. It was better to know the facts rather than image the worst. Greg opened the email and read it twice to make sure that he had understood it. The information in the email made him give a soft whistle in surprise. The last sentence of the report cleared up his concerns about Amanda's reasons for not talking about herself or making any close friends.

It would appear that his description of the Michaels' family had matched a missing persons report from the Philadelphia area. A woman and her two children had disappeared after a nasty divorce case had made all the local papers seven months ago. The judge had awarded total custody to the woman and put a restraining order on the husband who was known for his violent behavior and suspected connections to the syndicate. Some of the harassment details filled Greg with disgust.

He had always tried to observe tolerance in dealing with suspects regardless of the crime. Obeying his oath to protect and serve all the citizens had been easy for him, until today. But knowing that this man must have made life a living hell for Amanda had him seething with fury. He had a sudden desire to beat the man until he begged for mercy. Greg sincerely hoped that he never came face to face with Mr. Bradley Michaels because he wasn't sure he would be able to remember that he was a law officer. He closed the email and turned off his computer before leaving to pick up Sam and Sara from the diner.

Greg saw the kids as soon as he turned down Main Street. They were sitting on the steps of the diner with a duffel bag between them. They were eagerly watching the street. He might be totally fooled but he didn't think that pair was guilty of breaking any laws.

When Sam saw the patrol car park next to the diner, he opened the door and spoke to his mother. "Mom, Sheriff Greg is here."

Amanda walked out the door and approached the car. She smiled at the antics of Sam and Sara. They ran to put the duffel bag in the back seat of the cruiser and they were both trying to talk to Greg at the same time. It was impossible to understand more than one or two words. Greg looked a little overwhelmed as he tried to field all the questions they were asking.

"Thank goodness you're here. Sam and Sara have been pestering me for the last hour. They've been asking what time it was and whether or not you would remember to pick them up. They didn't want to be late getting to work."

"Of course, I'd remember to pick you up. My taxi service is very reliable. You can sit in the front with me and operate the radio." Greg told the children. He watched as they crowded onto the seat. They were so excited they were practically bouncing up and down trying to decide who would get to talk first.

"Sam? Sara?" Amanda waited until they stopped talking and looked out the window. "I want you both to mind your manners and remember that you're going to the tree farm to work, not play. Do exactly what Mr. Williams and Ms. Jones ask you to do. No arguing!"

"I'm sure the kids will do fine. Scott has a good rapport with children."

"Here's my cell number. Please tell Scott and Julie to call if they have any problems with the kids." Amanda handed Greg a slip of paper. She was smiling but her eyes held a look of apprehension that bordered on panic.

"Don't worry, Amanda. I won't let anything bad happen to them. You have my word on it. Enjoy your afternoon. I'll pick you up at your house at five o'clock." Greg held her hand an extra moment and gave it a slight squeeze to reassure her. He opened the car door, sat down and adjusted the seat belt before starting the engine and backing out into the street.

Sam and Sara returned her goodbye wave as Greg drove down the street. Amanda didn't know why but she knew in her heart that the sheriff would keep that promise. It was a tremendous relief to know that if anything were to happen to her, she could trust the welfare of the children to a man like him. He would make sure they were taken care of properly.

She turned out the lights and locked the diner door before walking to where her car was parked at the back of the parking lot. Out of habit, she checked the undercarriage of her car then raised the hood to check for anything that looked out of the ordinary. Then she cranked it up and drove home to repeat the search process there before running her bath water.

Amanda got out her expensive bath salts and fragranced candles. While the tub was filling up, she poured a glass of her favorite wine, put on some soft instrumental music, and lit the candles. She went into the bedroom, took off her work outfit, put on her silk robe and grabbed the mystery novel she had been trying to finish for weeks. Now, she was all set for a leisurely soak in a hot tub.

It had been so long since she had been able to relax and pamper herself that she wanted to take advantage while she had the opportunity. Greg was a truly wonderful man for giving her this carefree afternoon to be lazy. The wine and the heat of the water were making her feel so incredibly calm and totally feminine. The only thing that would make this scenario perfect would be if someone was there to join her in the bubble bath and scrub her back. *Maybe, I should have invited Greg home with me. I bet he'd know exactly what to do to make a woman feel better.*

As Julie stirred, rolled, cut and baked the dozens of cookies, she could hear the tractor going up and down the driveway. Scott was carting all the Christmas things stored in the equipment shed to the entrance area where the unadorned trees were waiting to be turned into works of art.

She took the last batch out of the oven and stopped to survey her handiwork. Trays of oatmeal, peanut butter, and sugar cookies shaped like trees and covered with colored sprinkles were on every available space on the kitchen counters. The aroma of baking cookies had pervaded the whole house making it smell like a pastry shop.

Julie checked the clock and decided that she had time for a quick shower before her aunt and uncle arrived. She was drying her hair when she heard a car drive up and park at the back of the house. Julie could hear Uncle John talking to Scott. Time to get lunch on the table.

Julie was putting ice in the glasses when Scott came in the patio door with Uncle John and Aunt Mary.

"I've set the lunch foods up buffet style on the counter. Help yourselves while I get the drinks poured. I have sodas and unsweetened tea." Julie took a quick glance at Scott. A slight blush covered her cheeks at the amused look in his eyes. "What would you like to drink?"

Scott wasn't sure why she was acting embarrassed. Before he could answer, they heard another vehicle pull up outside. Julie walked to the door just as Sam and Sara rushed up the steps onto the porch followed by Sheriff Rogers. She opened the door before they could knock.

"Come in. You're just in time for lunch. Go into the kitchen and make yourselves a sandwich," Julie told them. She watched as they sprinted through the living room. "Can you stay for lunch, sheriff? There's plenty of soup and cold cuts."

"Not today, thank you. I've got some work to finish before I can take the night off for the party. Here's Amanda's phone number if you need to call for any reason." Greg handed Julie the slip of paper with Julie's phone number. "But I will take a cookie or two as a delivery fee."

Julie darted back into the kitchen and put half a dozen cookies in a napkin. She handed them to the waiting sheriff with an indulgent smile. She didn't need a call to his mother to know that Greg loved cookies. The blissful expression as he took a bite was sufficient proof of that.

"Okay. We'll see you both later this afternoon." Julie tucked the paper into her jeans pocket and walked back into the kitchen.

Scott had observed this conversation and cookie exchange from the counter while he ladled himself a bowl of soup from the crock-pot. He was starting to think that he needed to have a serious conversation with the sheriff. Greg was a good friend but he needed to know that Julie was spoken for or she would be as soon as he could find time to get to the jewelry store.

For the next three hours the tree farm was busy with everyone scurrying around like a colony of ants. Scott and John were setting up the tables and chairs while Julie and Mary began sorting the decorations into categories according to the order they would be put on the trees. Sam and Sara were everywhere. They lugged cartons out of the storage shed and stacked them back inside when they were empty. The last box had been emptied and sorted when Scott waved the kids over to where he and John were putting up spotlights on top of the entrance sign.

"Take the wheelbarrow, load up the extension cords that are in the storage shed and bring them out here to me," Scott told them. They nodded their heads and took off in a race to see who could get there first. It must be nice to have that much energy.

"Scott, is the ladder still in the back of the truck? Would you get it for me? I need to adjust these lights to shine directly on the trees."

"Sure, I'll get it." Scott wondered what John was up to? They had placed those lights perfectly just a few minutes ago. He carried the ladder and placed it underneath the entranceway sign. He started walking toward his truck but stopped to ask John if he needed a screwdriver to make the adjustments.

He turned his head and caught John hanging a large sprig of mistletoe on the sign. He was placing it directly in the middle of the sign where everyone would be walking. John was a hopeless romantic.

For a minute or two Scott was tempted to tell John that the matchmaking efforts that Mary and he had engineered today were unnecessary. To let him know that as soon as he could get Julie to admit she felt the same degree of attraction, his intentions were serious enough to offer Julie his heart for a lifetime. Nah, that would take all the pleasure out of watching them throw Julie and him together.

Since Scott was also a hopeless romantic, he decided the mistletoe was an excellent idea. He'd have to make sure that he stopped Julie underneath the sign at the earliest opportunity. His smile was a little devilish as he let himself imagine all the possibilities that a kiss could lead to before the night was over.

Julie glanced out the window when she saw Sam and Sara raced toward the storage shed. They reached the open door at the same time and Sam declared it a tie. They started loading the packages of extension cords from the box into the wheelbarrow. Julie had moved some of the empty boxes to the back of the shed and was screened from their view. She was getting ready to call out to them when she heard Sam say something very interesting.

"If we work for Mr. Williams everyday until Christmas, we can earn enough money to buy that present for Mom that we looked at in the gift shop. We won't need to sell the things that we have stored in the old shed to the Secondhand Shop," he told Sara.

"But what will we do with all that junk we collected from the landfill?"

"We can just leave it there. People threw it away in the first place so it doesn't belong to anyone but us."

As Julie listened to this conversation, she realized that the kids hadn't been trying to steal anything from the farm. They were only trying to find a way to raise money for a Christmas gift for their mother. She'd talk to Scott about giving them a tree as a work bonus. Such unselfish love needed to be rewarded and they would need a tree to put that gift underneath.

CHAPTER FOURTEEN

Julie stopped and looked around the party area. The tables and chairs were arranged on the left of the entrance next to the buffet table that was laden down with a wide variety of food items. The hot cocoa was keeping warm on the serving tray and the coffee was perking, the rich fragrance mingling with the smell of fir trees.

Next to the twin trees scheduled for decorating, were two tables with enough garlands strings, tinsel, and ornaments of all shapes and sizes to decorate a half a dozen trees. Scott was placing mats over the extension cords to prevent the guests from tripping as they walked. Now all they had to do was wait on the local people to arrive.

Sam and Sara had worked hard all afternoon and were sitting at one of the tables eating candied apples. Judging from their sticky fingers and faces, the guests would need something to clean their hands after eating.

"Sam, I need one more thing from the house. When you finish your apples, go to the house and look in the pantry. You'll find a big container of moistened hand wipes. We'll need them for the guests to clean their hands." Julie smiled at him.

"Yes, ma'am," the answering grin on Sam's face showed that he knew it was a hint to clean their own faces and hands before they returned.

Scott watched as Sam and Sara walked toward the house. He might not know a lot about kids but those two didn't act like they were afraid of being caught red-handed stealing anything. They had both been very polite and followed his instructions without any signs of attitudes.

Like a magnet to a lodestone, Scott found his gaze returning to where Julie was making last minute adjustments to the food table. She was looking exceptionally beautiful tonight.

Mary had bought dresses reminiscent of the early 1900's for Julie and herself to wear. The green velvet dress had white fur trim on the collar, the cuffs and skirt hemline. Red leather half boots were visible beneath the long skirt when she walked. The olden style suited Julie. John and he had matching outfits of red plaid mackinaws and hats. Mary called it mood setting for the party. Mary and John were still at the house changing into their outfits.

This was the first time he and Julie had been alone all day. Scott decided that this would be the ideal time to give that mistletoe a chance to work its magic.

"Julie, can you come over here a moment? I need your help with something." He moved until he was standing in the driveway in front of the entrance sign.

As Julie walked toward Scott, she was thinking that he was even more handsome than usual tonight. The mackinaw and hat Mary had provided for the men to wear made him look like a lumberjack. He hadn't bothered to shave today and his beard stubble was a dark outline along his jaw that enhanced the rough and ready outdoorsman look. It was an extremely sexy look for a man who didn't need any help in that area.

"I've solved the mystery of the footprints. You'll never believe how harmless the tracks are. I overheard Sam and Sara talking earlier and they haven't been trying to steal anything from the farm. They've been collecting fixable junk from the landfill and storing it in that old shed up the road. They used the access road to keep from being seen by anyone who would tell their mother.

They were going to repair the things, sell to the Secondhand Shop in town and use the money to buy a Christmas present for their mother. Isn't that the sweetest thing? Just when you think today's children are spoiled and totally selfish, you meet some that show their love unconditionally." Julie's eyes were bright with unshed tears.

"Yes, that's nice. I'm glad that it wasn't anything more serious. I really like the kids." Scott smiled at Julie as she approached him. "It looks like everything is ready. I want to get a picture to commemorate all the work we've done but I can't figure out how this camera works."

Julie stopped next to Scott and looked at the camera he was holding. She saw the problem instantly. She took the camera, removed the lens cap and handed it back to him. She was going to make a teasing remark about him needing glasses when she noticed that he was staring at the sign above her head. She looked up to see what had captured his attention. Directly overhead was a large spray of mistletoe. She took a hasty step backward but Scott caught her hand in his.

He placed the camera on the table and pulled her closer to him. He put both hands on Julie's arms as he gazed into her eyes for a moment. The velvet material of her sleeves reminded him of the softness of her cheek when he kissed her last week. He caressed her upper arms as he waited for her to decide if she wanted to pull away. Scott was giving her the opportunity to object if she didn't want to be held.

"We shouldn't let John's special decoration go to waste." He bent down and touched his lips to hers. They tasted like sugar and spice. *And everything nice,* he completed the nursery rhythm in his mind. A lot like sugar cookies.

Scott intended it to be a casual, friendly kiss but everything changed when Julie placed her trembling hands on his chest and uttered a low, moaning sound. Scott responded by sliding his tongue over her lips to coax them apart. When she opened her lips slightly, he slipped his tongue inside and touched hers to see if she would respond. She quickly thrust her tongue against his in a ritual as old as time itself.

Julie moaned again and moved her hands up his chest to slide her fingers in the hair that was curling slightly in the dampness of the air. That caress made his heart start beating so fast that Scott thought it would explode in his chest. Julie's passionate response made his body harden instantly.

When it became necessary to take a breath, he slowly ended the kiss. The look in Julie's eyes made him pull her back into his arms. Their bodies matched perfectly. She was just the right height for her head to fit naturally on his shoulder. It felt so good to hold her body next to his. When he shifted his feet and pulled Julie closer, he couldn't tell whose heart was beating. His or hers. Two hearts beating in unison.

Julie closed her eyes and took a moment to enjoy the feel of Scott's arms around her. The reality of being in Scott's arms was so much better than her dreams. When Scott slipped his hand down from her waist to urge her hips into a more intimate position she could feel his arousal pressing against her body. Julie's body reacted with alarming speed. Pulsing heat was gathering in the pit of her stomach and her knees were starting to tremble.

Those instinctive signals sent her mind into major confusion. The emotional part of her brain wanted to ignore the upcoming party and invite Scott back to her house to finish what his kiss had started while the logical part cautioned her to take things slow. To be sure it was the right thing to do. If it turned out that Scott only wanted a quick fling, or even worse, a one-night stand, the business relationship between her uncle and Scott would be destroyed. As much as she wanted to make love to Scott, she didn't want to cause problems between them.

Scott heard a car door close softly and someone clear their throat. He turned his head to discover Greg Rogers and an attractive blonde woman watching them with amused looks on their faces. Julie and he had been so absorbed in each other that they hadn't heard the vehicle drive up and park behind them. Julie stepped out of his embrace and blushed. He buttoned his jacket and offered a quick thank you to the person responsible for the length of the jacket before he turned around.

"Welcome to Good Samaritan Tree Farm." Scott offered his hand to Amanda Michaels. "I want to thank you for allowing Sam and Sara to help us today. They went to the house to get something I forgot but they should be right back.

I'd like to introduce you to Julie Jones, who deserves all the credit for this special event. Julie, this is Amanda Michaels, Sam and Sara's mother."

"Hello, Ms. Michaels. It's a pleasure to meet you." Julie sent an indulgent look at Scott.

"Don't believe everything Scott tells you. He helped with all this planning, as well."

"It's a pleasure to meet you both and, please call me Amanda." She looked around at all the preparations. "Everything looks wonderful. You both are to be congratulated for all your hard work."

"Would you like some refreshments? We have coffee or hot cocoa and tons of food." Julie led Amanda to the buffet table to try to diffuse the awkward moment.

Scott watched as Julie and Amanda walked over to the refreshment table. Again he heard Greg clearing his throat to get his attention. When Scott looked at him, he grinned.

Scott returned the grin a little self-consciously. "We were just checking to see if the mistletoe was in the best spot for the customers. It works real well. You really should try it for yourself."

"As nice as that sounds, I need to keep my mind clear of that type of distraction." Greg didn't tell his friend that he was having enough fantasies without having the memory of what kissing Amanda felt like running through his head.

"From the look in your eyes, I'd say things are heating up between you and Julie. That's an interesting development but you might want to tone it down a bit. People will be here soon and they'll be jumping to conclusions if they catch you looking at Julie that way. You know how fast gossip spread in this town."

"You're right. I don't want anything to jeopardize my chances in any way."

"Did the kids seem nervous or anxious today?" Greg asked.

"No. They were just your normal, noisy kids enjoying the outdoors and helping as much as possible. They reminded me of my sister and me when we were that age. Besides, Julie overheard the kids talking today and the mystery of the footprints has been solved. The kids have been collecting junk, storing it in the old shed across the road and using the access road as a shortcut. They thought they could to sell some of it to the Secondhand Shop to earn money to buy their mother a nice present for Christmas. The only real harm is the danger they exposed themselves to by being out in the middle of night. It makes my blood turn cold just thinking about the bad things that could have happened to them."

"When I drive them out here after school next week, I'll have a serious conversation with them about their nocturnal activities. Scare tactics usually work with that age group." Greg and Scott's attention returned to Julie and Amanda as they stood talking at the buffet table.

"Greg, do you ever seriously think about settling down and starting a family?" Scott asked his friend. "We aren't getting any younger you know. If we wait much longer, we'll be too set in our ways for any woman to put up with us."

"Funny you should mention that. Lately, I've been wondering what it would be like to come home to a home cooked meal and someone to share it with. I'd like to open the door and say 'Honey, I'm home' and know that someone would be there with a hello kiss," Greg replied as he followed Scott's line of thought. "If things get too lonely, I guess we could get ourselves a dog. They don't care how grouchy you get or if you leave muddy tracks on the floor when you come home late."

"That's true but a woman has other talents besides cooking and cleaning," Scott told his friend with a gleam in his eyes.

"I agree." His eyes followed Amanda as she and Julie stood at the tables.

Amanda had on a pair of jeans that had been washed until they look soft and comfortable and she had layered an oversized sweatshirt over a blue-denim shirt. The casual clothing made her petite figure look feminine and very appealing. Soft and cuddly. He wanted to hold her in his arms and assure her that most men weren't lowlifes like her ex-husband. If she'd only confide in him, he could protect her and the kids from any dangers, real or imagined. But first, he needed to gain her trust.

Scott turned his head and started to say something but the look in Greg's eyes as he observed the ladies standing at the buffet table made him stop. He smiled as he realized that he wasn't the only man to be hit by Cupid's arrow this holiday season. Valentine's Day was over two months away but it looked like the rascal had been shooting arrows at his best friend, too.

CHAPTER FIFTEEN

The decorating party was going well. Holiday music was playing from the stereo Scott had set up on the tailgate of his truck. People were laughing and talking as they put the lights, garlands, and ornaments on the twin trees. Jason Clark, the Spencer Star photographer, was snapping pictures of the activities from every angle. He had caught several couples underneath the mistletoe as they celebrated their love for each other with a quick kiss.

The children were especially happy because they were getting to decorate one tree all by themselves. The noise level from a dozen little voices was deafening. Everyone was talking at the same time as they placed the ornaments with careful detail to the color coordination. Scott and Greg had even helped them by lifting the children up so they could hang ornaments on the branches they couldn't quite reach. Julie and Amanda were complimenting the kids on their tree being the most beautifully decorated tree they had ever seen.

All evening Greg's eyes had been irresistibly drawn to Amanda. She was having a great time. She was acting as young and carefree as Sam and Sara. Julie and she were helping the children by giving suggestions for the placement of the ornaments. Amanda had suggested that each child have an equal number of ornaments by tagging them with the children's names. That way they all could feel like they had helped.

"Greg, I need your help over here for a few minutes," Scott requested from the opposite side of the party area. He was working on the light connections stand between the trees.

"Sure thing. I'll be right there." Greg handed Amanda the box of ornaments he had been holding while Sara picked out one with her name on it.

"I'm going to help Scott for a few minutes but I'll be back to help put the star on top."

"Thanks. I was wondering how I was going to hold the ladder steady and climb at the same time."

"I'll do the ladder climbing, okay?"

"No argument from me. I wasn't looking forward to getting that high," Amanda told him with a relieved sigh. "I'll sit here and rest until you're through helping Scott."

Greg walked over to the table where Scott was trying to get the electrical connections ready for the tree lighting. It contained the heavy-duty extension cords that ran to each of the decorated trees and connected to one switch for a simultaneous illumination.

"What seems to be the problem?" Greg asked.

"I forgot to bring an female adapter for this connection. John went to look in the equipment shed but I think I remember seeing one in the toolbox in the back of my truck. I'd go look myself but I have a couple of more wires to connect. There's a flashlight on the front seat."

"I think I can handle that. Just be sure you connect the right wires. That's high voltage you're holding in your hands."

Greg retrieved the flashlight and began the search. It didn't take long to find what he was looking for. He closed the toolbox and carried the adapter to Scott.

"Here you go, old man. Need anymore help?" Greg asked even though he was anxious to get back to Amanda.

"Yes, I do. Can you hold this flashlight while I get this last wire connected to the switch? It'll just take a minute."

Scott quickly finished and stood up. He slapped Greg on the back and together they headed over to the refreshment table. Greg would get a hot cup of coffee before he headed back over to help Amanda with that star. His glance toward the tree confirmed that she was waiting as promised but she was helping Sam with an ornament.

"Mom, it's time to put the star on the tree. Can I do it?" Sam asked.

"I don't think you can reach it, honey. Sheriff Greg promised to help put in on the tree for us. He went to help Scott but he'll be back soon." Amanda told him as she took the box that contained the star from Sam.

Amanda looked around but she couldn't see Scott or Greg anywhere. She decided to take the ornament out of the box while she waited. Surely, he'll be back soon. It didn't take long to pull the glittering star from the box.

"Mom, is Sheriff Greg going to come soon?" Sam asked his mother. "Everyone's waiting for the star to be put on top so we can turn on the lights."

"I guess I'll have to do it for you." Amanda stood up and went over to place the ladder next to the tree. "Sam, do you think you're strong enough to hold the ladder while I climb up?"

"Let me help steady the ladder for you, Mrs. Michaels" one of the gentlemen standing nearby offered. He was standing in a shadow so she couldn't see his face very well.

"Thank you," she told him as she began to climb up the rungs of the ladder to put the big star on the tree. She was going to have to climb all the way to the top of the ladder because the top part of the tree was just out of reach. Being short was such a disadvantage when you had to reach high places.

Amanda stood on her tiptoes and stretched as high as she could. She had just reached up to put the star in place when someone bumped the ladder. The ladder swayed and Amanda tried to grab the top rung but her hand missed and she toppled toward the ground. She screamed as she watched the ground getting closer and closer. All the people standing around the buffet table gasped as they watched in horror.

When they heard a scream, Scott and Greg turned quickly to see what was happening.

Greg pushed several of the bystanders out of the way and leaped forward. He caught Amanda just before she hit the ground twisting so his body would cushion her fall. They landed in a heap of tangled legs and arms with a loud thump.

Greg held Amanda for a second or two to catch his breath before he stood up and placed her in one of the chairs lining the refreshment table. Sam and Sara ran up to the table with eyes as big as saucers. Sara climbed up into her lap and began to cry. Sam's chin was trembling in his effort to keep his own tears from falling. Instead, he put his arms around his mother and hugged her tight. Joe and Maggie Bosley came hurrying up to help comfort the children and check on Amanda.

"Are you okay? What in the world were you doing climbing up on that ladder? You could have been badly injured." Greg shouted. His heart was racing wildly because that had been a close call. If he hadn't been standing so close, he wouldn't have been able to reach her in time.

"I'm sorry. I know I should've waited for you," Amanda's voice shook in reaction to the near tragedy. "The children were getting impatient about getting the star put on top. Everything was fine until I reached the top rung. I thought that man was holding the ladder but suddenly, I was falling. I don't know how it happened."

"What man? Where is he? I have a few questions I'd like to ask him." Greg asked in a deadly serious voice as he looked around. The glint in this eyes indicated that the conversation wouldn't be polite.

Amanda looked around nervously at the people standing around the party area staring at her in concern but didn't see the man anywhere. "I don't see him. He had on jeans and a denim jacket."

"Honey, a lot of the men have on jeans and jackets. Do you remember anything unusual about him? Anything that would set him apart from the crowd?" Greg asked.

"The only unusual thing about him was the boots he wore. They were made of very expensive ostrich leather." Amanda replied. She looked around at the people staring at her. "Please, go on with the party. I'm fine."

At Greg's nod, Scott announced that it was time to light the tree. Scott went over to the control panel. In an effort to lighten the mood, Scott gave an exaggerated drum roll and with the touch of a switch, both trees were blazing with hundreds of tiny lights.

The two trees were a beautiful sight with all the decorations and the stars in the sky as a perfect backdrop. Everyone applauded and cheered. The photographer took several shots of the lighted trees before he began packing up his equipment.

The townspeople made an effort to get the mood back after Amanda's near accident but after a few minutes, they began to say goodnight to Scott and Julie with promises of returning the next afternoon to buy a tree. Within minutes, everyone had left except the Michaels family, John and Mary Jones, Greg and Scott. Amanda was seated at the table with an arm around Sam and Sara trying to reassure them that she was all right.

Greg and Scott were standing next to the entranceway talking about the incident and trying to figure out what had happened to make the ladder topple so suddenly. Greg told Scott about the denim-clad gentleman that Amanda had mentioned.

"There were several men in jeans and denim jackets but I didn't notice those boots on any of them. Did Amanda recognize him as someone she had seen from the diner?" Scott asked.

"No, but she looked more frightened by the idea of a strange man than the fall itself. I need to have a serious talk with her," Greg said in a determined tone of voice. "I've got to find a way to convince her that I'm sincere when I offer to help. Women can take the independent attitude too seriously. If she has a problem or in some kind of trouble, I want her to know that the sheriff's department can help solve the situation."

"I'm sure you'll find a way if you put your mind to it," Scott replied with a puzzled look at Greg. He appeared very disturbed by the possible threat to Amanda. Greg's agitation sounded like he had a personal interest at stake, instead of being the county sheriff. Scott hoped Greg wasn't getting in over his head with Amanda.

Greg sensed that Scott found his concern a little excessive and tried to rein in his anger.

In his profession, he had observed that most of today's women didn't understand that a man still needed to know that he could protect them from the predators of this modern world. It was an intricate part of a man's persona and was a large part of what attracted women to them in the first place. Then they proceeded to try and change him into sensitive companions.

117

Men had the same habit of being attracted to the "hot babes" but never trying to get to know their minds or the beauty of their souls. Then they'd become jealous when they thought other men viewed them the same way. To combat these feelings, the men tried to control the woman's life, even their friends. Making them think that they were coming on to the other men and then becoming abusive in their efforts to control the situation. Both sexes needed to understand and accept their God-given differences and learn to love each other, warts and all.

Greg walked over to where Amanda and the children were. "Are you ready to go home?"

"Yes, please." Her legs were shaking so badly Amanda hoped she could make it to Greg's vehicle before her knees gave way.

Greg called goodnight to Julie and Scott before helping Amanda to his Jeep. Sam and Sara followed closely behind them.

* * * * *

The darkness of the forest was excellent camouflage for the man crouched low to the ground watching the chaos that had erupted as soon as the ladder tipped over. The sheriff had moved with a speed that he hadn't thought possible in such a crowded area. He hadn't tarried after he had pushed on the brace to make the whole thing collapse. He had barely made it to the edge of the road before they had begun looking for the mystery man. He wished they'd break up the party soon. It was damp and cold behind this fallen branch.

CHAPTER SIXTEEN

During the drive into Spencer City, Greg and Amanda were both quiet, lost in their own thoughts. Greg looked at the kids in the rear view mirror. They were sound asleep. All of that running around must have tired them out. That was good because he intended to ask Amanda some more questions about the "accident" and the mystery man.

"Do you feel like talking about the ladder incident?" he asked in a quiet, soothing voice. "Or is something else bothering you?"

"I'm not sure if it would be wise to involve someone else. Some problems from the past seem to have followed me here. The problems are linked to my ex-husband and his family," Amanda responded in a voice that was weary and resigned. Her hands were clasped tightly in her lap.

While he tried to think of the right thing to say, Greg reached over and covered her hands to reassure her. He wasn't prepared for the jolt of awareness that he felt. He quickly removed his hand and placed it back on the steering wheel. He needed to keep his mind on business.

"We can keep this off the record between friends or I can listen in a sheriff's capacity? I can help if you'll let me," he told Amanda.

"I'd like to discuss it but can we do it in a couple of days after I've had time to calm down a little bit? I don't want to fall apart in front of the kids," Amanda asked in a voice that trembled. "I'll need to call my attorney in New York before I discuss the situation about my ex-husband."

"Okay, that's fair enough. Just remember that problems are easier to bear if they're shared," Greg told her as he drove up and parked in front of her home. He helped her carry Sam and Sara into the house and waited in the living room while she put them to bed. When Amanda came back, he was staring out the window into the darken neighborhood.

"Thank you for taking us to the decorating party. Except for the ladder incident, we had a good time," Amanda told him with a smile that didn't quite reach her eyes. "Your quick reaction saved me from getting badly hurt."

"You're welcome. It's good to know I've still got my old football playing instincts. Try to get some sleep and call me when you're ready to talk," Greg replied as he flexed his arm that had hit the ground. It was going to have a bad bruise tomorrow. "Will you be alright here alone? Do you need me to stay awhile?"

"I don't want to put you to anymore trouble tonight. I'll be fine." She walked with him to the door and locked up after thanking him again.

Amanda watched from the window as Greg got into his vehicle and drove down the street. She turned off the lights and went to bed. She lay in the darkness and tried not to let the fear overwhelm her. To not let it make her run away from a town that had begun to feel like home. She had made some good friends here. The friendliness of the people was one of the reasons she loved it here. They honestly cared about the well being of their neighbors.

Greg didn't tell Amanda that he intended to keep a watch on her house tonight to make sure the unknown man hadn't followed them. There wasn't any conclusion evidence that tonight's ladder "incident" was an attempt on Amanda's life and as far as he knew there hadn't been any verbal or written threats. It was just a gut feeling he had.

After reading the bureau's report on her husband, he couldn't take any chances. It wasn't part of his job as sheriff to act as a bodyguard to keep Amanda safe but he knew that he'd be devastated if he didn't do all he could to protect her from this danger. She needed someone to watch her back and he was volunteering for the job.

Greg drove out of view of Amanda's front windows and parked. He radioed the deputy to meet him on the corner of Pike and Stone to keep an eye on the street while he got a thermos of strong coffee and some sandwiches would help him make it until morning.

Scott and the Joneses' spent the next hour loading the leftover food and decorations into Julie's SUV. While Julie and Mary took the food back to her house, John and Scott folded up the tables and chairs and loaded them onto a trailer. He had to return them to the community center tomorrow.

Scott found himself staring in the direction of the storage shed where he could see the women unloading the boxes of decorations. That kiss earlier had surprised him in its' intensity. His brain was torn between a desire to repeat the occurrence as soon as possible and fear of the complications a relationship might cause between the partners. Especially if Julie wasn't interested and turned him down. He was so preoccupied that John had to ask him something twice before it penetrated the fog in his mind.

"Even thought the fall from the ladder caused a little more excitement than we planned, I think the official opening of the business went well. It was very fortunate that the sheriff has good reflexes or the young woman could have been injured badly." John handed Scott the last stack of chairs.

"I think Amanda was more shaken up than hurt. Julie and I'll check on her to make sure that she's okay. The people seemed to enjoy the party atmosphere of decorating a community tree. Because of Julie innovative planning, I think the Good Samaritan Tree Farm is well on its way to being a success."

John drove the tractor toward the shed where the two women were waiting to help with the unloading.

Mary couldn't help but notice that Julie was unusually quiet as they watched the tractor slowly advancing up the driveway. "The community party was a hit, don't you think. The kids really got into decorating when they discovered they had a tree all to themselves."

"Yes, it was a good way to launch the business. Tomorrow's sales will be best indicator of whether it was a success or not." Julie was only half listening to her aunt's conversation. She was thinking about the man riding on the back of the trailer. She didn't know exactly when it happened but Scott had broken through all the invisible barriers she had erected around her heart like a F-5 tornado. Stirring up all her emotions until she couldn't think clearly.

Mary knew something was bothering Julie. She was responding to her remarks with an absentmindedness that was uncharacteristic. It must be something very important for her to be so distracted. It could be the fall Amanda had experienced but she wasn't sure that would cause this level of thoughtfulness. Julie was a grown woman and didn't always confide in her like she did when she was a teenager. All she could do was wait and hope that Julie found a solution to whatever was bothering her.

John drove the tractor and trailer into the shed and parked it for the night. "It's been a long day for old folks, so Mary and I will say goodnight and let you youngsters finish unloading all these extra decorations."

"Goodnight, John. I'll see you tomorrow before you leave."

It didn't take long for Scott and Julie to place the last boxes inside. Now that they were alone, he was having difficulty putting his thoughts into words. *If I only knew whether her reaction earlier was simply lust or honest attraction, I could take a chance and tell Julie how much I care for her*, his inner voice of reality told him.

Julie was restacking boxes that didn't need it in an effort to give her nerves time to calm themselves. The tension was thick enough to cut with a knife. She sneaked a peek at Scott and saw him peeking at her. He grinned like a little boy caught with his hand in the cookie jar.

How can he look so adorable and sexy at the same time? Just the memory of those kisses made her stomach muscles tighten with desire again. Don't think about how good those lips felt when he kissed you or you'll never make it into the house tonight.

"It's getting late. We'd better get some rest. Tomorrow will be busy with customers coming to buy Christmas trees." She started walking toward the doorway.

Scott stopped her with a gentle touch on her arm. "I think we should talk about what happened between us earlier. Can we have coffee tomorrow after John and Mary leave?"

He was absently rubbing his thumb across her wrist causing a shiver to run up her arm.

She couldn't resist the impulse to touch him. She placed her free hand on the side of his face in a tentative caress. His beard was even heavier now and it created a friction as she rubbed gently.

His tender look of yearning deep in his eyes made her smile. She tiptoed slightly and placed a soft kiss on those sensual lips.

"Lunch will be at eleven-thirty since Uncle John and Aunt Mary want to leave by twelve o'clock. Come join us and we can talk afterwards." Julie responded to his question. She tugged her hand gently away from Scott, turned and continued walking toward the house.

"Goodnight, Julie. I'll see you tomorrow."

Julie stopped and turned to look back at Scott. "Yes, it will be a good night because I'll be dreaming about you and how good it felt to be in your arms. The only arms I want to hold me," Julie said with a come-hither look.

Before Scott could recover from the shock of that remark enough to react to the invitation in her eyes, she winked and blew him a kiss before sprinting toward the house. Scott watched until she closed the door. Only the fact that her aunt and uncle were staying overnight stopped him from following her. He turned off the lights and locked up the storage shed.

As he walked home, he kept hearing that last remark of Julie's. He wished there was someone around to pinch him just to make sure that he wasn't dreaming. She had definitely cleared up those doubts of his. He felt like shouting his joy to the heavens. It was amazing how happy you could be when the person you loved thought you were wonderful too.

When he got home Scott didn't bother turning on any lights to get a glass of water from the kitchen before going to bed. In the darkness, the blinking light on his telephone answering machine caught his attention. He switched on a light and pushed the retrieve button to identify the caller's phone number and time it was recorded.

What would Greg Rogers be doing calling him at this hour? Scott listened intently as he heard the sheriff's message.

"Scott, I'm calling to alert you to a possible situation with Amanda and her kids. I have reason to believe that the ladder incident tonight wasn't an accident but a murder attempt. I'll be on a stakeout at Amanda's house tonight to make sure there isn't another attempt made. I just wanted to let someone else know in case something should happen to me. I'll call first thing in the morning to let you know more details."

Scott listened to the message twice more to make sure he was hearing correctly. It was incredible to think that such a heinous crime would be perpetrated against such a nice woman. Even hardier to believe was the fact that it was happening in a community where the worst law-breaker was a petty thief or an occasional hunter poaching game out of season.

Scott debated calling Julie to make sure they locked the doors securely. He decided that it would only cause unnecessary alarm. It would be best to wait and get more information from Greg tomorrow. But just to be on the safe side, he got his pistol down from the top shelf in the hall closet and placed it along with a box of cartridges in the nightstand next to his bed.

* * * * *

In a nearby motel room, a man stood looking out the window and wondered how much to tell his client when he called in to make a progress report. He sat down on the bed and picked up the phone and dialed. After punching in his cell phone number, he added 911, which was the sign to call ASAP. It was after midnight but he didn't have long to wait. He answered his cell phone after only one ring.

"I've found them. I arranged a little "accident" tonight but someone prevented it from being a permanent one," he told the man on the other end of the phone line. "She seems to have acquired an unofficial bodyguard, but I'll catch her alone sooner or later."

"That's good news. Just remember that there's a deadline and you don't get paid unless it happens before then. I've had some of the local cops hassling me about my business suppliers so I need to keep our contact to a minimum in case they decide to search my phone records. I don't want them to trace you back to me so don't contact me again until it's over." The man hung up the phone and smiled to himself. If everything went as planned, he would have total control of all that money by New Year's Eve.

CHAPTER SEVENTEEN

The first official day of tree sales for the Good Samaritan Tree Farm was very successful. As soon as church services were dismissed, the local townspeople were true to their promise. There had been a steady stream of customers ever since noon. Residents from the neighboring towns had come to check out the new business. Julie's advertising had done the trick.

Even Anna and Angelo Venetti had driven from New York to buy a tree. They were as excited as Sam and Sara as they went in search of the perfect tree for the wine shop. Scott smiled at the odd picture Angelo made as he shouldered the tree saw and he marched down the rows of trees with Anna. He had offered to drive them on the cart but Angelo had wanted to wander around before making his selection.

Scott was putting a tree on the shaker machine to remove the dead needles when he heard a squeal of delight from the parking area. He turned around in time to see Julie hugging a young woman in a bright green parka. They were laughing and talking at the same time. He didn't recognize the woman. It must be one of Julie's New York friends.

"Aimee, this is a wonderful surprise. How did you get the day off?" Julie asked and hugged her friend again.

"There was no way I was missing this special day. I convinced my boss that a fir tree in the lobby would be a good way to spark the public's interest in the upcoming museum tours. Instead of regular ornaments, we're going to put miniature envelopes containing free tickets for the tours that the elementary schools are sponsoring. Besides I had to come collect my free tree." Aimee looked around at the size of the trees and frowned in consternation.

"What brought on that look of bewilderment?" Julie asked.

"I just realized something. My little compact will look like a rolling forest creature if I try to get two trees that big on the luggage rack."

"Don't worry. Scott can put protective netting around them really tight and they'll both fit just fine." Julie reassured her.

"Okay. So, my friend, where is this hunk I've heard so much about. Are you still having all these conflicting feelings about him?" Aimee watched as Julie's eyes widened and she smiled broadly.

"I'm not confused any longer, Aimee. He is the most incredible man. I get goose bumps just thinking about him. It's hard to believe that we only met a few weeks ago. I can't wait for you to meet him. That's Scott loading the tree onto the station wagon." Julie smiled and waved her hand at him.

Aimee looked over toward the area where Julie was waving. A large man was lifting the huge fir tree like it was a feather. He had taken off his jacket and his t-shirt was clinging to muscles that rippled as he moved. Aimee raised her eyebrows and grabbed Julie's arm in a fake fainting spell.

"If the rest of the men wandering in these woods look like him, then I'll be a frequent visitor. The ones I meet at the museum are stuffy professor types in tweed jackets and only discuss the best lighting for their one-man show or a studio portrait."

Scott observed the visitor as she stood beside Julie. She must be the roommate from college that Julie had mentioned. It was hard to believe that someone who appears so vivacious was Julie's best friend. At Julie's wave, he walked over to where they were standing.

"Scott, this is Aimee North. Aimee this is my new boss, Scott Williams."

"Hello. Welcome to Good Samaritan Tree Farm. It's good to meet you. Julie mentioned that you would be coming by for a tree. Just pick one out and I'll be happy to load it for you. Do you see anything that fits your needs?"

"It's good to finally meet you, Scott. Julie's told me so much about you, too, but I thought she was exaggerating. Are there any trees that will fit on my midget car that won't covering it completely?"

"Julie, why don't you let John show Aimee the special section. There's a row of smaller trees at the back that should be perfect. She can tag them with a white ribbon and I'll go cut them as soon as I help Mr. Venetti."

"That's a good idea. The special section has the best trees and it'll be good to have our trees seen by the buying public in New York. I'll walk Aimee to the house. Uncle John went to check his email." Julie linked her arm with Aimee as they walked toward the house.

As soon as they were out of hearing distance, Aimee spoke. "Julie, if you don't grab that man while you have the chance, you'll be making a huge mistake."

"I totally agree with you. As soon as the season is finished, I'm going to let him know that I'm willing to risk anything for a future with him."

Scott finished helping Mr. Venetti's cut down his tree, placed in on the cart and started back toward the tree farm parking area. They had reached the entrance just as a large motor home pulled in and parked. Scott smiled when he recognized the couple inside. The man coming down the steps was an older version of him and right behind him was his mother. He parked the tractor next to the tree shaker and went to greet them.

"Mom, I was beginning to think you had changed your mind about coming to the grand opening." Scott caught his mother up in a bear hug and twirled her around before setting her back on her feet. He turned to shake his father's hand while his mother berated him for being so juvenile.

Thomas Williams shook his head and laughed at them. He looked around the area and nodded his head in satisfaction. His boy had done it. Scott had made his dream of owning a tree farm business come true and judging from the trees lashed to the cars they had met while driving from Spencer City it had been a good first day.

"Scott, everything looks great. I especially like the decorated trees. It gives the entrance a festive holiday feel."

"Thanks, but I can't take credit for them. That was Julie's idea. She's a great ad man. That's her standing next to the payment stand." Scott told his parents.

Thomas looked in the direction Scott had indicated. Julie had chosen to wear a pair of jeans and one of the T-shirt's that she'd had designed for the tree farm. The logo was a miniature of the entrance sign. The outfit was enhanced by the curves it covered.

"If you think that's a man, son, I'm going to have your eyes checked out by the nearest ophthalmologist." The smile of appreciation on his face for the picture Julie made as she waited on the customers was suspiciously like his son's.

"Thomas, close your mouth before you start drooling. Scott will think you've never seen a pretty woman before. Never mind your father. When do we get to meet her?" Anne Williams asked her son. It would take more than a pretty face to convince her that this woman could make her son happy.

"Right now. Here she comes," Scott replied.

Julie knew immediately that the couple Scott was greeting so enthusiastically was his parents. The older man's features were a clear giveaway. Except for the salt and pepper hair, the gentleman looked exactly like Scott.

"Hello, I'm Julie Jones. It's good to meet you. Scott told me you would be coming by to visit before going to Florida. Can I get you something to eat or drink?"

"No, thank you. We stopped at Joe's Diner earlier for a piece of his delicious apple pie. But I would like a tour of this special section that Scott has described in his emails." Anne told the young woman.

"Of course. I'd be happy to show you Scott's achievement. It's not that far so we can walk there easily. It will give us a chance to get acquainted while Scott visits with his dad. We'll be right back." Julie smiled at the look of concern on Scott's face as she escorted his mother down the driveway.

"Don't look so worried. Julie looks like she can take care of herself." Thomas told his son. "Now, show me how this shaker device works."

Mrs. Venetti and Scott's mother had been talking to Julie and Aimee while they waited for Angelo and Scott to tie the tree on the top of the Venetti car. Scott had gotten the impression that they were discussing him because the four women had looked over at him several times and laughed like conspirators. It wasn't much telling what embarrassing story those two women were telling Julie about him.

When Julie and he had been saying goodbye to the Venetti's, Anna had said something that was a little bit puzzling.

"Thank you for coming today. It was nice to meet old friends of Scott's. I hope you will visit often." Julie had told them.

"We don't get the chance to get away from the shop very much but we'll be sure to send a special bottle of wine for the celebration," Anna had replied with a twinkle in her eye.

Scott must have missed something from the earlier conversation. He couldn't remember any celebration plans that they'd discussed. He would have to ask Julie later what Anna had meant. But right now he had to get Sam and Sara safely home.

That thought reminded Scott of the conversation he had with Greg Rogers earlier in the day. The things he had learned about Amanda's ex-husband made a cold chill run up his spine. Greg and he had decided on a plan of action. They were going to keep a watch on the Michaels family 24/7 until Greg had a chance to investigate the "accident" fully. Greg was sticking close to Amanda when she was at home and Scott was making sure that he was with Sam or Sara when they were at the tree farm.

Greg and he had also decided that the less people to know about the threat the better so for now he wasn't discussing the situation with Julie. It would be better to go about the tree farm business as usual so they didn't scare off any suspects. He was going to be paying attention to the footwear of all his customers, particularly the customers that he didn't recognize.

Scott pulled up into Amanda Michaels' driveway behind the sheriff's cruiser. He waited until Amanda opened the door before letting Sam and Sara out of vehicle.

"We'll see you tomorrow afternoon, kids. It's only three more weeks until Christmas."

"We may be a little late tomorrow. Sheriff Greg is taking us by the jewelry store before we go to the tree farm, Mr. Scott? We've saved enough money to buy a special gift for Mom," Sam told him with an excited look in his eyes.

"Take as much time as you need. Goodnight, kids."

Scott backed out into the street and drove off toward home checking out each car that passed him on the street. It was a little nerve-racking to be constantly on the alert for suspicious persons but it would be worth it to keep those two kids from losing their mother.

CHAPTER EIGHTEEN

Today was the big day, Christmas Eve. The donation trees and all the decorations were loaded on trailers ready to be taken to the selected locations. The past three weeks had passed in a flurry of activity. Between the tree farm, getting to know Julie better and helping Greg with the protection plan for the Michaels family, Scott hadn't had a many extra minutes to think about his own special plans for later tonight. But the anticipation was building with each tick of the clock.

Tree sales had been better than either Scott or John had expected but that was only an added bonus to this special season. Despite the tension he felt inside, the best part of this holiday season had been discovering that the love he felt for Julie was mutual.

They had spent the days selling trees and the nights discussing their plans and dreams for the future. Their goodnight kisses had been filled with so much passion that it had made it difficult to leave her house and go home to his empty bed each night. He wanted to wait until they were officially engaged before making love to Julie, so he had taken lots of cold showers and made plans to make this Christmas with Julie the first of many. Scott shook his head to focus his attention on the day's plans.

John and Mary were in charge of nursing homes while Julie and he were set to deliver their share of trees to three orphanages. They had several pairs of volunteers to help with the decorating, including the Michaels' family.

Part of the donation plan was for each child to have a present for Christmas. The Boone County Sheriff's Department had been responsible for collecting the toys or contributions to buy them from the local businesses. Sam and Sara had gotten into the holiday spirit by donating part of their hard earned money to help buy presents for the kids in the orphanage. Sam had told him that since these boys and girls didn't have a mommy or daddy, he wanted to be sure that they knew that other kids wanted to make their Christmas special. The presents weren't the only surprise the kids were going to have this year. Scott had arranged for a Santa Claus to stop by at each orphanage.

Last night all the volunteers had gathered at the courthouse to wrap and tag each present. It had looked like an east coast annex of the North Pole by the time all the gifts were wrapped and stacked in the boxes ready to be put on the trailers for the trip to the orphanages.

After they had cleaned up the scattered remains of colorful paper and ribbons, the group had sang along with the Christmas carols playing on the DVD player Julie had brought with her. Then they had stopped to enjoy the large pot of his chili, a tray of sandwiches and a dozen of his famous apple pies from Joe's Diner.

"Have you given out cameras to the volunteers?" Mary asked Julie. "I want lots of pictures to capture the look of wonder on the children's faces and the joy of being a part of the celebration for the senior citizens."

"Yes, each pair of volunteers has a camera and several rolls of films ready to record the festivities. I want to use part of them to make an advertisement collage for next season. Scott and Greg will drop the trees and decorations off at the nursing homes then they'll go on to the Children's Home," Julie assured her aunt before turning to address the volunteers.

"Does everyone have the maps with the assigned locations marked?" Julie asked the group of people who were getting ready to begin this journey of hope and love. The drivers of each vehicle replied with a honking of horns and waved their direction sheets. "Any questions? Good. Let's get this show on the road."

The trucks pulling the trailers moved slowly out of the drive followed by six cars filled with the sounds of joyful voices lifted in song. It looked like a modern day version of the tax-payers journey to Bethlehem.

The trees donated to the nursing homes had brought laughter and smiles of joy to everyone involved. The relatives of the senior citizens had expressed their appreciation of everyone's efforts with smiles and promises to help with the volunteer effort next year.

Because for a little while that day, their mothers, fathers, aunts and uncles were happy and excited to be celebrating this special holiday with people who loved them. The presents were only everyday items needed by the elderly residents but as Mary watched them being opened with childlike enthusiasm, her eyes filled with tears.

John smiled at her and placed an arm around her waist to pull her up close to him. He leaned down to whisper in her ear. "Are those tears of joy or sorrow?"

"A little bit of both. Joy because our plan is working so well. I'm glad that we can fill this day with such simple pleasures for them. Also, a little bit of sorrow and anger that so many don't have their own families here to celebrate with them."

"Hopefully, we can make this something they can look forward to each year." John took her hand and together they began to visit with the residents. Complimenting them on their new gifts and getting smiles and hugs in return. Those smiles made all the time and effort involved in making this happen worthwhile. Better than money.

The children's eyes at the orphanages had been filled with happiness as they helped decorate the trees. Later, when Santa Claus had arrived with a bag of presents slung over his shoulder, they had been filled with awe and eager anticipation. Even the older kids who didn't really believe in Santa were excited as they opened their gifts.

Scott watched as Julie showed a little girl how to stir up a brownie mix and set the timer on a toy oven. She was doing everything she could to make this a memorable Christmas for the children. She looked up to catch him looking at her and winked at him. She bent to say something to the young cook who smiled shyly and nodded her head. As happy as he was to be a part of this special mission, Scott was anxious to get his own tree trimming plans underway.

The children had opened the last of the presents, the cookies and milk were finished and it was finally time to go home. After hugging the children, wishing them a Merry Christmas and Happy New Year, Amanda and Julie gathered up their handbags and went outside to join Scott and Greg who were waiting outside with Sam and Sara. Greg was taking Amanda and her children in his Jeep while Scott drove Julie's SUV home.

"Merry Christmas," Julie hugged Sam and Sara and told them that they were the best workers.

"I put a couple of extra gifts in their backpacks. Will you make sure they're under your tree tomorrow morning?" Julie asked Amanda.

"Yes, I'll take them out after they go to sleep. I can't thank you and Scott enough for all you've done for my family. May God bless you," Amanda couldn't stop the tears that formed in her eyes. Julie's eyes were a little damp, too.

"Okay, Greg. Time to go before the girls get too emotional." Scott remarked. "I've got big plans and want to keep this a happy evening."

Scott dropped Julie off at her house and went home to change clothes and get the special present he had bought for Julie. He picked up the red velvet box that was sitting on his dresser. The box was in the shape of a star ornament and contained a diamond solitaire ring. It was a simple marquis cut but represented all the love he felt for Julie.

Since he planned on waking up next to Julie in the morning, Scott had insisted that they only needed one tree. Together they had picked out the perfect tree yesterday and he had placed it in the corner of her living room earlier today. Tonight after decorating the tree, he planned on asking her to marry him.

Two steaming mugs half-filled with wassail were setting on the coffee table along with a plate of cookies. A fire was burning in the fireplace, lamps were dimmed low, and Christmas carols were playing softly as Julie debated with him over the best placement of the red, gold and silver ornaments. They had hung the handmade ones that she had been collecting through the years carefully on the tree. Finally, the last strand of tinsel had been placed strategically and it was time to turn on the tree lights. Scott switched off the overhead light and sat down on the sofa beside Julie to admire their joint efforts.

"The tree looks marvelous, if I do say so myself. We make a good decorating team." Julie smiled at Scott. "Would you like some more wassail?"

"In a few minutes. I have one more ornament for the tree and I need your opinion on the best place to put it." He went to get the box he had left in the pocket of his jacket he had hung up in the hall closet. He returned to the sofa and handed the red velvet star with the gold cord to Julie. Now that the time had come, he didn't know exactly how to express all the things he was feeling.

"What a beautiful and unusual ornament? It's a little heavy so it will have to go on a strong branch." Julie observed as she studied the tree to locate the perfect place for it.

"It's heavy because it has something special on the inside. Open it and tell me what you think."

Julie opened the star. Inside was a beautiful diamond ring and a card with three simple words printed on it, I love you. The eyes she raised to meet Scott's were beginning to fill with tears but the smile on her face was a happy one.

"Julie, I realize we've only known each other for eight weeks and three days but I fell in love with you the first time I saw you standing in John's doorway. I want to make all your dreams and wishes come true. Will you marry me and make this holiday the beginning of our life together?" Scott took the ring out of the box and placed it on the third finger of her left hand.

Julie was so overcome by her emotions that she couldn't speak for the lump in her throat.

She could only nod her head yes in acceptance of the most romantic proposal anyone had ever received and pledged her love with a soft kiss as the tears coursed down her cheeks.

Scott wiped them away gently and placed a kiss on each eyelid. He placed soft kisses on her face until he reached her lips. Julie quickly looped her arms around his neck and gave him a kiss that left them both trembling with excitement and thinking about other ways to celebrate their engagement.

"Scott, I love you so much. You have filled my life with so much happiness. Just being here in your arms will make my dreams complete. I'm going to send a dozen roses to Aunt Mary as a thank you for her matchmaking efforts and to let her know that she had excellent taste when it came to finding me a husband."

"Are you sure there isn't anything special that you wanted for Christmas? We can send Santa an email before he leaves the North Pole." Scott asked her.

"Actually, I did have a special Christmas wish that I wanted Santa Claus to bring to me tomorrow morning."

Julie whispered something in his ear that made him sweep her up into his arms and start walking toward her bedroom.

"Your wish is my command." That was one Christmas request that Scott intended to fulfill immediately and he wouldn't need Santa's help.

CHAPTER NINETEEN

The next morning, Scott awoke slowly to the realization that the soft, warm body curled up next to him was real. He closed his eyes for a minute then opened them again to make sure that he wasn't still asleep and having one of his vivid dreams. He turned his head to look at the woman sleeping beside him. Julie was so incredibly beautiful. Although it was nice that her facial features and perfect body were part of the complete package, it was the beauty of her spirit that he loved most. A love that went all the way to his soul.

They hadn't gotten a lot of sleep. Whenever one of them had moved in their sleep, it would wake up the other bed partner. Those wakeful periods had led to kisses then making love again and again. As much as he wanted to wake Julie up and celebrating their engagement one more time, Scott decided to let her sleep a little while longer while he fixed something special for breakfast. But first he needed a strong cup of coffee.

Scott was humming the wedding march as he moved about the kitchen. He wanted to make this Christmas morning the first in a long line of traditions for the new future they were beginning. He would start by serving Julie breakfast in bed.

He opened the bottle of champagne that he had stashed in the refrigerator last night and placed the bottle along with two crystal flutes on a tray with bowls of strawberries and cream. Now he was ready to serve breakfast to his lady love and discuss exactly when the wedding would take place. He wasn't sure if he deserved all this happiness but he offered up a prayer for all the blessings of this Christmas morning.

Scott walked into the bedroom and quietly set the tray on the dresser. He sat down on the edge of the bed and began tracing the outline of Julie's ear with his finger. Such a delicate ear. Julie stirred and rolled over but didn't awaken. She was sleeping so deeply that drastic measures were needed to get this breakfast feast underway. He started placing kisses on her bare shoulder and worked his way up to that sensitive spot behind her ear that he had discovered last night, along with a few others.

Julie opened her eyes to find Scott propped on one elbow with a devilish look in his eyes. A slow smile appeared on her face as she looked up into those chocolate brown eyes.

"Is this how you usually wake up your lady friends or is it something you've reserved for fiancées only?" Julie asked as she placed a quick kiss on Scott's lips.

He thought about that question for about thirty seconds before answering. "That sounds like a leading question and I believe I should take the fifth and consult an attorney before I say something that could incriminate me. What time will your aunt and uncle be up?"

She glanced at the bedside table to check the time. The LCD readout was seven o'clock.

"They're probably up but I think we should let them have their coffee first before we call to let them know about our wonderful news. Do you think Uncle John and Aunt Mary will be pleased?"

"I hope so but that's not why I want to call him. Even though technically he isn't your father, he's been the person who willingly took over those responsibilities and deserves the traditional honor of giving his blessing.'

"Uncle John will be so happy that you're making that gesture. Has anyone ever told you that you are a beautiful man? I can't believe how lucky I am to have found you."

"No, but it's nice that you think so. But before we make that call, I want to start a new tradition just for us. Champagne and strawberries are waiting to be served to madam," Scott informed Julie in his best butler voice.

They managed to eat the strawberries and drink a glass of champagne between kisses.

Kisses that led to caresses that led to love making. The champagne was a little flat by the time they got around to drinking it but neither one of them minded in the least. When Julie had taken the last bite, she announced that it was time to place that call to New York.

"Let's make the call on the speaker phone in the office so we can talk and hear what's being said together. I'll join you as soon as I take this to the kitchen." Scott picked up the tray and walked toward the door.

Julie held her hand up to admire the sparkle of the diamond as the lamplight hit the stone. She hopped out of bed and put a robe on before going into the office and dialing her uncle's phone number. She was sitting on the desk swinging her feet like a little girl on a swing.

Scott entered the office, sat down in the desk chair and pulled Julie onto his lap as they waited for the phone to be answered. When they heard John say hello, Julie spoke first. "Merry Christmas, Uncle John."

"Merry Christmas, Julie."

"Is Aunt Mary there with you?"

"Yes, she's sitting across the table. Do you want to speak to her?"

"Not yet. I have you on the speaker phone because Scott has something to ask you."

"Good morning and Merry Christmas, John."

"Merry Christmas. What's so important that you have to call and discuss it this early on Christmas morning? Is there a problem with the tree farm?"

"No problem. Julie and I have some news that we wanted to share with Mary and you.

During the past month, we discovered that while being friends is a nice relationship, we wanted to make it something a little more permanent. Last night Julie agreed to be my wife. We'd like to get your blessing on the marriage." Scott slipped his arms around Julie's waist.

"Scott, that's the best news I've heard since Mary accepted my proposal. You have my permission to officially become a member of our family. The blessing will be having you as a nephew." Scott and Julie could hear John telling Mary the news, then an excited shriek that made them wince in pain from the pitch. Mary immediately took the phone from John.

"Julie, I couldn't be happier because I think Scott is such a special person. I've always considered him a part of our family and now it will be the truth. Have you discussed a wedding date and what kind of ceremony you want?"

"No, we're still in a state of euphoria. And I totally agree with you. Scott is a wonderful man. To celebrate our engagement, he fixed me a special breakfast complete with champagne and served it to me in bed." Julie told her before she realized exactly what she was admitting.

"That sounds very interesting, dear. I didn't know that Scott had such a romantic imagination." Mary heard Scott chuckling and saying something about being inspired.

"Come to dinner tomorrow evening so we can welcome Scott to the family properly.

Enjoy the rest of your day and we'll see you tomorrow. We love you, Julie. You, too, Scott."

"Dinner sounds wonderful. We still have to call Scott's sister and parents in Florida so we'll talk more tomorrow night. I love you and Uncle John, too. Goodbye." Julie hung up the phone and gave Scott a tender kiss.

"Julie, look." Scott pointed to the window. Outside, snowflakes were silently falling to cover the fir trees and turning the Good Samaritan Tree Farm into a beautiful winter wonderland. "It's going to be a white Christmas after all. I wish everyone could be as happy as we are today."

EPILOGUE

Molly Hampton glanced out the window at the snow-covered countryside. Watching the snowflakes drifting down was so peaceful and serene. As if the craziness of the world was taking the day off to remind everyone of the promise of a better future.

The motel dining room was almost deserted with the exception of one man sitting at a table watching the wind whirling the snow against the glass panes of the window. The middle-aged man didn't appear to appreciate the winter scene he was looking at through the window because the look on his face wasn't very pleasant. As the waitress went to refill his coffee cup, she noticed that he was jotting notes down in an appointment book.

"Would you like dessert to go with your coffee? We have fresh apple pie and blueberry cobbler a la mode."

"Sure. I might as well. My car doesn't have chains so I can't drive in this weather," he told her in a disgusted voice.

While he waited for the waitress to return, the man tried to analyze the situation by reading his notes. Woman is never alone. There are too many witnesses at work. Always accompanied by friends at night.

There were only six days left. He couldn't go home until the job was finished. His client had instructed him not to harm the children but if he didn't get a break soon, he would be forced to use them as bait to get the mother alone.

Plus, the situation was becoming more hazardous every day. The longer he stayed around town the more likely that people would remember his face and the price of failure was too high. It wasn't healthy to botch an assignment in his business.

ABOUT THE AUTHOR

Writing has been a dream of Breanna's since she wrote her first short story for English Literature class in high school. When she turned fifty, she decided to get a Liberal Arts degree. A Creative Writing course inspired her to start writing again. Her favorite memories of childhood are going with her father to cut down a tree to bring home and decorate with ornaments. She set this novel during the holiday season because the spirit of love that surrounds the holiday season brings out the best in people. Breanna loves to celebrate with family and friends by giving and receiving the gift of love and friendship, which is the best gift of all.

Printed in the United States
18737LVS00004B/226-234